CONTRADICTIONS

CONTRADICTIONS
Yang Gui-ja

Translated by
Stephen Epstein and Kim Mi-Young

East Asia Program
Cornell University
Ithaca, NY 14853

The Cornell East Asia Series is published by the Cornell University East Asia Program (distinct from Cornell University Press). We publish affordably priced books on a variety of scholarly topics relating to East Asia as a service to the academic community and the general public. Standing orders, which provide for automatic notification and invoicing of each title in the series upon publication, are accepted.

If after review by internal and external readers a manuscript is accepted for publication, it is published on the basis of camera-ready copy provided by the volume author. Each author is thus responsible for any necessary copy-editing and for manuscript formatting. Address submission inquiries to CEAS Editorial Board, East Asia Program, Cornell University, Ithaca, New York 14853-7601.

Korea Literature Translation Institute grants supported the translation and publication of this book. The cover design by Richard Hahn was made possible by a donation from Mr. and Mrs. I.H. Cho.

Number 126 in the Cornell East Asia Series
Copyright © 2005 by Stephen Epstein and Kim Mi-Young. All rights reserved
ISSN 1050-2955
ISBN-13: 978-1-885445-36-0 hc / ISBN-10: 1-885445-36-9 hc
ISBN-13: 978-1-885445-26-1 pb / ISBN-10: 1-885445-26-1 pb
Library of Congress Control Number: 2005922987
Printed in the United States of America
23 22 21 20 19 18 17 16 15 14 13 12 11 10 09 08 05   9 8 7 6 5 4 3 2 1

⊗ The paper in this book meets the requirements for permanence of ISO 9706:1994.

CAUTION: Except for brief quotations in a review, no part of this book may be reproduced or utilized in any form without permission in writing from the author. Please address inquiries to Stephen Epstein in care of the East Asia Program, Cornell University, 140 Uris Hall, Ithaca, NY 14853-7601.

Contents

	Introduction	vii
1	Into the World with a Cry	1
2	Lies	11
3	A Human Landscape	21
4	My Father, at Melancholy Sunsets	43
5	Indistinct Shadows of Love	53
6	The Meaning of Those Ten Minutes, Long, Long Ago	67
7	Wallowing in Misery	81
8	Sweet Ju-ri	91
9	On the Road to Dosol Hermitage, Seonun Temple	99
10	Three Memos about Love	113
11	A Fourth Memo about Love	115
12	Unbearable, All Too Unbearable	121
13	The Day After We Parted	133
14	Christmas Present	141
15	Bittersweet	151
16	A Letter	155
17	Contradictions	161
	Afterword	167

Introduction

We start, in essence, with a stop: please don't read the entire introduction quite yet. An unusual request for a preface, perhaps, but so be it. After all, the book you are holding is titled *Contradictions* (Mosun, 1998), and Yang Gui-ja, who in her author's afterword expresses the hope that readers may encounter her novel unhampered by others' impressions, would appreciate the irony. Nonetheless, those approaching the text in English should be equipped with at least a modicum of the background Yang would have taken for granted in a Korean audience. I therefore first provide some information on Yang Gui-ja and the contemporary literary scene in Korea, at which point readers mindful of the author's wish may move to the text itself before returning here for discussion of the novel proper.

Yang Gui-ja's writing career has now spanned some twenty-five years, and in that time she has established herself as one of Korea's major literary figures, with a succession of literary prizes and best-sellers to her credit. A native of Jeolla Province, Yang (b. 1955) debuted with "Dasi sijakhaneun achim" (Morning Begun Anew, 1978), a short story that earned her the year's Newcomer Award from the influential journal *Munhak sasang* (Literature & Thought). In the early stages of her career, Yang's fiction focused on the psychological traumas experienced by average Koreans as the nation plunged forward on the path of development. Her most representative work *Wonmidong saramdeul* (The People of Wonmidong, 1987) is a compilation of loosely interconnected short stories that explores the social upheavals engendered by Korea's careening rush into modernization, industrialization and urbanization.[1] In a series of pieces initially published in literary journals between 1985 and

---

1. *Wonmidong saramdeul* is now available in English in a fine collection titled *A Distant And Beautiful Place*, translated by Kim So-young and Julie Pickering (University of Hawai'i Press, 2003).

1987 and subsequently collected into an extremely popular single volume, Yang depicts the lives of the residents of Wonmi-dong, a district in Bucheon, one of the satellite cities of Seoul that developed rapidly during the 1980s. Yang, herself a migrant to the capital, draws on her own experience as a resident of the neighborhood for these imaginative tales and portrays the effects of radical social change with sympathy, irony and poignant flashes of humor.

The stories in *Wonmidong saramdeul* also often obliquely suggest the brutality of South Korea's authoritarian regime and its dehumanizing effects on the Korean populace. This concern continued to find expression in Yang's fiction in the late '80s and early '90s. Her 1993 collection *Seulpeumdo himi doenda* (Even Sadness Becomes Strength), for example, contains the story "Cheonmachong ganeun gil" (The Road to Cheonmachong, 1988), which criticizes the government's appalling human rights record. Also available in that anthology is the novella "Sumeun kkot" (Hidden Flowers), the 1992 recipient of the Yi Sang Prize, one of Korea's most prestigious literary awards. The swift domestic and international changes of the late 1980s suddenly turned the world upside down for Korea's left-leaning intelligentsia, and in this autobiographical narrative, Yang threads her way through the labyrinth of confusing thoughts she found herself wandering in at the time. Writer's block, a trip to a Buddhist temple, the collapse of socialism in Eastern Europe, meditations on inner strength, and memories of Korea's difficult years of military dictatorship all intertwine in an examination of an author's relationship to historical circumstance.

Her first full-length novel *Huimang* (Hope, 1991) uses a wide cast of characters to interrogate contemporary values, setting those who have borne the brunt of Korea's modernization drive against exemplars of bourgeois shallowness and offering the promise of reconciliation. The pioneering—and best-selling—*Naneun somanghanda naege geumjidoen geoseul* (I Desire What Is Forbidden Me, 1992) offers a feminist revenge fantasy in which the protagonist, a woman pursuing graduate studies in psychology, kidnaps an idolized actor. Yang has been increasingly exploring psychology at a personal rather than social level, however. Her even more successful follow-up novel, *Cheonnyeonui sarang* (A Thousand-Year Love, 1995), is an unabashed love story, but one with a twist: a young couple who were unable to bring their love to fruition in a previous life meet once again, reincarnated, in a tale that attempts to convey traditional Eastern sentiment in modern guise. Yang has also continued to garner critical acclaim with such novellas as *Gom iyagi* (A Bear's Tale, 1996) and *Neup* (The Swamp, 1999), the recipients of the Hyeondae Munhak (Modern Literature) and 21Segi Munhak (21st Century Literature) Prizes, respectively.

Taken as a whole, Yang's career has been marked by diversity and the search for new challenges. Among her writings are several collections of essays. Additionally, she has published a novel for children, *Nuriya, nuriya mwo hani* (Nuri, Nuri, What Are You Doing?, 1994). Perhaps most intriguing is a different sort of creative endeavor: Yang's native Jeonju is well-known in Korea for its cuisine, and in the mid-'90s she opened a restaurant in the trendy Hongik University district in Seoul. This foray into business also led to *Bueoksin* (The Kitchen God, 2000), a work in which she turns her literary talents to describing the rewards and tribulations of life as a restaurateur.

One should, of course, also view the various developments in Yang's writing within a wider context of political and social trends. The Republic of Korea in the early twenty-first century is vastly different from what it was when Yang embarked on her literary career. In 1978 memories of a devastating civil war colored daily life, and rabid anti-communism dominated national ideology. Although Park Chung-hee, who was to be assassinated in 1979, had overseen a period of swift export-led growth, poverty remained rife. The 1980s were a stormy decade that began with the military coup of Chun Doo-hwan and the ruthless suppression of citizen protest in Gwangju, a city in Yang's native Jeolla Province. Years of iron-fisted rule and equally determined opposition followed; throughout it all Korea's economy continued to grow at an extraordinary pace. Mass protest in 1987 saw the middle class take to the streets along with students and laborers to demand greater democratic participation in the decision over Chun's successor. Chun was eventually forced to give in to pressures for a direct election, and he stepped down from power shortly before the 1988 Olympics put Seoul on the world stage. And although his hand-picked choice, Roh Tae Woo, still became the next president when the opposition candidates split the vote, the success of the protest represented a turning point in South Korea.

The 1990s witnessed the election of both the nation's first civilian leader in Kim Young Sam and the first peaceful transition of power to an opposition party with the inauguration of Kim Dae Jung. The Roh Moo Hyun presidency has shown even greater promise of political reform. South Korean democracy may have had a troubled birth and a tempestuous adolescence, but one can now argue without difficulty that it has truly matured. The institutions of civil society and concern for the rights of the individual have become ever stronger. Moreover, despite the financial shocks of late 1997, which Yang refers to indirectly in her afterword to *Contradictions*, per capita income in South Korea has continued to grow. The vast majority of the younger generation now know poverty only as a distant memory of the country's past. The juggernaut of the Korean economy may have been temporarily slowed by the so-called "IMF Crisis," but it surges forward, and the national mood overall can be considered to remain optimistic. Globalization has become a buzzword in Korea during the last decade, and internet usage ranks among the highest on the planet. Although Yang was born into a war-torn land that was one of the globe's poorest, today there can be little question of remarkable success: South Korea has taken its place as a major nation in an increasingly interconnected world.

All these changes have necessarily had an impact on the country's literature as well. While exact statistics can be difficult to come by, it is clear that by any standards the South Korean public reads a great deal and takes its writers seriously. In a nation of roughly 45 million, literary works, including volumes of poetry, sell over a million copies with regularity. Moreover, Korean authors have not shied away from issues of importance. South Korea has often witnessed vigorous debate among its writers and critics about the value of pure literature versus that which is, first and foremost, socially engaged. In the '90s, however, with a steadily mounting portion of the population established in the middle class, and overt political oppression retreating further and further into the background, literature took a notable turn towards the personal. With this inward turn has come a growing diversity of subject and styles, and a change in readership patterns. Poetry has increasingly yielded in popularity to novels. Political and social injustice is no longer the primary theme of Korean literature, a change lamented by some and championed by others. A didactic streak runs deep in Korean literature (evident in *Contradictions* in many of the pronouncements from the narrator, Jin-jin), and those who value literature above all as a vehicle for moral improvement fear its degeneration into mere entertainment.

As tastes have changed, older writers once popular have fallen somewhat out of favor, and new, younger authors have taken their place. Many of these new authors are women, who have now assumed a leading role in the literary world. Some, such as Yang herself and compatriots Choe Yun, Gong Ji-yeong, and Kim In-suk, have explored in their fiction what it means for those politicized during the '80s to come to grips with a world in which ideology has lost its meaning. Among female writers who have risen to recent prominence, Sin Gyeong-suk has received the most critical attention. Her work is marked by a sustained examination of the psyche and concern with psychological dislocation, a condition Sin has termed "internal exile." In a lyrical style, Sin often focuses on the theme of painful love, but her talent lies in treading this minefield of potential triteness with pointed emotional analysis and conveying an intimacy that allows readers into the minds of her protagonists. Not surprisingly, the majority of these protagonists are female. Traditionally in Korea there has been a sharp division between male and female spheres of activity, and Korean literature writ large, although often deliberately blurring the boundaries between these spheres, reflects a society in which men's interests are public/political, while women's are private/domestic. More and more, however, the protagonists in Korean fiction engage with the vicissitudes of their own individual lives, rather than serving as representative Koreans who have experienced internecine warfare, national division, grinding poverty, dictatorial government, and class injustice.

How, then, to read *Contradictions* within such a social and literary context? We turn now to the novel itself and flag a pause for those who first wish to encounter the story unencumbered by the remarks that follow. *Contradictions* was Korea's best-selling work of fiction in 1998, the year of its publication, and has remained a steady seller since. In this coming-of-age tale Yang explores the paradoxes and contradictions of the human condition, and delves into the meaning of love, marriage and personal happiness. The opening chapter sounds the keynote: An Jin-jin, the first-person narrator, awakes one morning with a determined cry to devote all her energy to her life. Her struggle over whom to marry informs the novel, as the text contemplates how easily such a decision can determine one's fate, a fact impressed upon Jin-jin by the divergence she has witnessed in the lives of her mother and her mother's twin sister.

Readers will immediately perceive the multiplicity of binary oppositions that appear throughout the novel, starting with Jin-jin's mother and aunt, and Na Yeong-gyu and Kim Jang-u, the two men who are courting her. We also encounter opposition between Jin-jin and her cousin Ju-ri; Jin-jin's brother Jin-mo, the wannabe gang boss, and her cousin, Ju-hyeok, the Ivy League graduate; Jin-jin's father, an alcoholic (and apparently schizophrenic) vagrant who thinks too deeply about things, and her uncle, a steadfast, rigid architect. At first these oppositions may seem so schematic as to reduce the story to modern-day fable. And, in part, as Yang implies in her afterword, the novel deliberately sets out stark antitheses in order to draw universal lessons from the set of lives that revolve around An Jin-jin. Nonetheless, Yang is too talented a writer not to problematize the oppositions that she sets up. To say more would detract from the enjoyment of the story for those who have persisted on in this introduction, but suffice it to say that the dichotomy between the weepy mother and silk-pyjama-clad aunt of the first chapter is by no means as blatant as initially suggested, and that the opposition between Jin-jin's father and her uncle is replayed with interesting twists in the decision she must make between Kim Jang-u and Na Yeong-gyu. Readers should also not forget that the notion of complementarity runs deep in the yin/yang philosophy of East Asia. The title itself, *mosun* (contradiction), is a Sino-Korean word built from the characters for spear and shield, with which we conclude each chapter. The term evokes the dynamic interaction of opposing forces, as hinted by the parable at the end of the work.

Yang's writing has long combined such antithetical emotions as desperate grief and hopeful optimism.[2] In the past, however, interest in contradiction had spurred her to probe *sahoe gujojeogin mosun*, the contradictions inherent in social structure that create strife between the wealthy and the working class, as in her short story "Bi oneun narimyeon garibongdonge gaya handa" ("On Rainy Days I Have to Go to Karibong-dong"). Sociopolitical concern, a hallmark of Yang's writing elsewhere, is almost entirely lacking in this novel. Early on Jin-jin explicitly rejects such larger frameworks as an explanation for her life, in fact, when she says "I don't particularly trust people who pin the responsibility for everything on family or society or the system." One of the novel's own contradictions, however, is that by eschewing politics, it serves as a valuable index of current Korean society and can be regarded as a representative novel of the late 1990s. Those who have read much Korean literature in translation will be aware that texts treating Korea's difficult political and social realities have often been first to make their way into other languages. Such readers may well find *Contradictions* refreshing, precisely for its greater universality, and a view of the nation that is less relentlessly solemn. Except for place names and patterns of behaviour firmly rooted within local mores (albeit ones that are rapidly changing), *Contradictions* does not, in the first instance, obviously rely upon a Korean political and social background.

The attentive will nonetheless be able to discover much about contemporary Korea in the novel. Jin-jin's "Three Memos About Love," in chapter 10, portray the manifestation of that emotion in terms of consumer capitalism: telephones, pop songs, cosmetic concerns before the mirror. Narrative details conjure up a world of TV dating shows, CD stores, Sunday drives, computer training institutes, atmospheric cafes, smoky barbeque joints, and pretentious French and Italian restaurants. Despite Jin-jin's references to her family's poverty, such poverty is clearly relative and not absolute; she and Jang-u, who is seen as struggling with equally straitened circumstances, readily manage a weekend getaway to a mountain tourist resort in a car that Jang-u owns. Jin-jin therefore offers no critique of an oppressive and unjust socioeconomic system. Rather, she inhabits a world in which social mobility is entirely possible: her family's unfortunate circumstances are seen as a result of *unmyeong* (fate) and her father's character flaws. Her cousin Ju-ri insinuates that the key problem is that he has shirked his responsibilities; had he been different, perhaps Jin-jin too could live in an affluent neighbourhood, go

---

2. Cf. Hwang Do-gyeong, "Babui jinsilgwa noraeui jinsil" (The truth of rice and the truth of song) in Yang Gui-ja, *Wonmidong saramdeul* (Munhakgwa jiseongsa, Seoul, 1997), p. 370.

on shopping sprees, and earn a doctoral degree from the United States. And although Ju-ri's voice is certainly undercut within the text, we have travelled far from the underlying Marxist view of class that tinted much literature from the '80s, including Yang's own.

Contradictions does, of course, retain characteristic traits of Yang's writing in its vividly drawn characters, its attention to structure, its ironic touches—and, like her earlier work, it simply makes for an engaging read. How do we account, though, for the presence of a very different ethos? In "Hidden Flowers," mentioned above, Yang describes her fall into a state of creative despair. With socialism discredited as a viable alternative, she had found it difficult to find protagonists for her stories, and she realized that she had been operating within a narrow artistic sphere. In a not dissimilar way, Jin-jin early on relates her despondency over the shallow dimensions of her life and laments how observation of her mother and aunt had instilled in her a fatalistic lack of motivation to investigate her own life carefully. Nonetheless Jin-jin finds the impetus to begin her examination anew, as Yang Gui-ja did. Yang's epiphany in the earlier novella comes with her recognition that the actual business of living one's life concretely should take precedence over ideology. This simple truth enables her to move onward as a writer in the '90s and to find literary possibilities amongst life's "hidden flowers." (The deep emotion Kim Jang-u experiences when he comes upon hidden wildflowers evokes an intertextual resonance with Yang's prize-winning piece). Likewise, Jin-jin's realization that there is no shame in analysing her own family as a means of understanding herself allows her to engage in the self-examination she had previously rejected.

And yet. I have emphasized a growing movement in Korean literature away from more traditional public concerns, but for all the text's concentration on individual fulfillment, *Contradictions* ultimately invites a political reading as well. How, the work asks, is it possible that Jin-jin's mother and aunt, twins in their early fifties, could have become so radically different? Anyone with even the barest knowledge of the Korean peninsula might well ask a similar question on a collective level: how is it possible that North and South Korea, two nations born slightly over fifty years before the novel's publication, from the same genetic material and the same womb of history, could now be travelling such widely divergent paths? Whether or not Yang Gui-ja intended her work to address such a question, the issue of national division remains ever present in the Korean imagination, continuously percolating at a subconscious level and regularly bubbling up into popular discourse. Readers will have to decide for themselves how far they want to push allegory. Might we draw an analogy, for example, between Jin-jin's uncle, a train that brooks no deviation from its schedule, and the determined push to progress of authoritarian regimes in the Republic of Korea? Can Ju-ri and Ju-hyeok's rejection of their homeland for life in the United States be read within a larger framework of South Korea's ongoing Westernization? To what extent are we to see Jin-mo, the prodigal son, a womanizing, movie-loving, petty gang boss, confined within a prison of his own making and unable to distinguish between fantasy and reality, as a doppelganger for Kim Jong Il? Questions worth pondering.

Finally, a brief note on our transliteration of Korean: in this volume, my co-translator Kim Mi-Young and I have opted, for the first time, to follow the new government Romanization system rather than McCune-Reischauer, the favored system of scholarly practice.[3] We do not wish to enter into the pros and cons of what is often a heated debate, but will merely note that our choice was ultimately determined by a simple factor: the name of the protagonist appears as Jin-jin in the new system and Chin-jin in McCune-Reischauer. We find the former rendering both more readily suggestive of the doubling of characters in her name and more aesthetically appealing. We hope readers agree.

Stephen J. Epstein

---

[3]. Readers should note, however, that we follow author's preference for her own name and thus print *Yang Gui-ja* rather than the expected *Gwi-ja*.

1 Into the World with a Cry

We think others' unhappiness is natural.
Our own unhappiness, though,
We can never accept.

One morning I cried out the moment I woke up. Suddenly. No divine revelations, no prompts from elsewhere. Cross my heart.

"Enough! I can't go on living like this! I've got to make every second of my life count. That's exactly what I've got to do!"

And if you'll let me use the phrase "cross my heart" one more time, I don't usually sound like I'm caught up in intense introspection. Not at all. What's more, I have nothing but contempt for people who get all histrionic. I cast them aside without a second thought.

That morning, though, I cried out not once but twice: I've got to devote my life to *me*. And while I was puzzling over what I had done, something even stranger happened. Without warning, tears rolled down my cheek, one by one.

At first I thought it had rained during the night and that our feeble ceiling was leaking again or that maybe I had been agitated and sweat had beaded up on my face. Honestly, that's what I wanted to believe. But no. They were tears.

If it hadn't been for the tears, I probably would have forgotten my outburst, ignored it as part of a dream I had on the verge of waking up. If it hadn't been for the tears, I wouldn't have felt any responsibility for the passionate call to action that forced its way from my lips. Words can come out of nowhere. It's not hard for me to ignore my babble when I talk to myself.

But here was stark proof: a final teardrop clinging like dew to my eyelashes; a moist Kleenex; a heart heavy with a dull, lingering ache. The evidence weighed upon me. Come on, out with it. Explain yourself. And clearly.

One of my strong points is that I do my best to satisfy requests that are made of me. The anxiety I caused my mom by running away from home once in junior high and twice in high school? All a result of this trait of mine.

When I was in junior high my brother asked me to buy him new sneakers, so I left home and worked for two months in an Incheon hat factory. At first I planned to settle the sneaker problem by working for a month during summer vacation, but I got greedy. Two months later I made a triumphant return, with sneakers for my brother and me and even leather shoes for my mother. Of course, despite bringing shoes home for the whole family, I still met with a savage beating and unstinting abuse from my mother. But I was paid back in full for the contempt she heaped on me—whenever she went out on special occasions, she wore the shoes I bought her.

Both of the times I ran away in high school were because of friends' requests. My best friend left home first and another friend followed. I grew bored all alone, and when things got dull for them, they'd call and ask me to come and hang out. The first time I went to liven things up for them lasted a week; the second time was a little longer—a month. I just thought of it as a long outing. I never swore to stay away or anything like that. Maybe home was tedious, but it wasn't as tedious as life is.

My motivation for running away may have been trivial, but the result was anything but. No matter what I did, the term "runaway" stuck; it colored how people looked at me. Later on it came to capture my essence as a human being. I can't count how often I overheard people criticizing me behind my back. "That silly girl ran away three times . . ."

So after I turned twenty I never once explained what happened—until now. I realized instinctively that you have to protect yourself. People aren't capable of savoring all the twists and turns of another's life, only sneering at them. Even when what has happened is amusing and not just amazing.

Anyway, one March morning when the flowers were in bloom, I was suddenly overcome by a request of my own. Explain who you are. Why not? So I've decided to put everything in order, beginning with the most basic items. I can't think of the tiniest reason to hide anything about my life, average as it is. Here are the particulars:
Name: An Jin-jin.
There. I'm Jin-jin. My parents agreed to use a single syllable in naming me, Jin—"Truth." But on the way to the district office to register my birth, my father changed his mind. That's my dad. He could take ages to reach a decision, then five minutes of sober reconsideration would make him flip-

flop. And so he decided to change my name on the spur of the moment. Dad said to the staff member, "If you write a character like Jin just once, it feels too serious. Let's double it up. If I have other daughters, I'll name them "Seon-seon" and "Mi-mi."[1]

There never were any other daughters, though. And even my father never noticed that our family name "An" came first, a syllable that can also be understood as meaning "not." If you want to overinterpret a bit, you could say my fate has been to go through life denying my name.

Age: twenty-five years, seven months.

Family: mother and younger brother, one each. You could add my father, a bum, who used to come home every now and then but doesn't any more.

As for my education, I'm taking time off from university for the very simple reason that I had to get together the huge sum necessary for my fees. Of course, if I were thoughtless enough to pester my mother for money or knocked myself out working part-time, I wouldn't have to take leave so often, but what'd be the point? I have nothing to do and I've still got five good years left in my twenties.

It would waste a lot of time to run through all the jobs I've had since taking a leave of absence from school. If I'd had to explain my employment history just two or so months ago, I'd have hesitated a bit and then had to answer "service industry." I manned the cash register in a cafe with a lazy owner and constantly wound up having to serve cups of tea to mere kids. The term "service industry" would have fit perfectly.

Fortunately, though, I can now respond "office worker." How do I like the job? Well, even though I've saved enough money for a semester's tuition, I put off applying for readmission this March. If there's one thing that bothers me about the job, though, it's that my own efforts to get it were useless, while a single sentence from my uncle dropped in passing worked wonders. He solved the problem with one phone call. All he needed to say was, "We don't have any places open in our company."

Interests: none.

I don't particularly like the word "interests." As far as I'm concerned, it's usually just shorthand for "dubious interests." When it comes to what people really enjoy, questionable pastimes way outnumber respectable ones. The owner of the cafe claimed his hobby was classical music: he said he could listen to it anytime, anywhere. Actually, his hobby was seducing married women. To put it in his words, it didn't cost anything, wasn't dangerous, and

---

1. The triad of *jin* (truth), *seon* (goodness) and *mi* (beauty) entered Korea from the realm of Kantian aesthetics and has come to be upheld as an ideal of femininity by such institutions as Ewha Womans University.

it gave him an adrenalin rush. The only problem with it as a hobby was that he couldn't openly include it on his resumé.

The value of my assets that I'm able to declare publicly is 428,000 won. If you promise not to let on to my mother and younger brother how much I'm really worth, I can whisper that I've actually got ten times more than that. I don't think building up a bank account is a principle to base your life around, but I know better than any of my peers just how important money is. Sometimes when people are making a deal or doing business, they look all serious and say, "Money isn't the important thing." I don't believe it for a second, though. That kind of talk is a trick. Everyone knows that the important thing *is* money.

I could add several other items about myself. For example, I'm neither tall nor short, neither repulsive nor stunning, I've read a variety of books, and I know something about this and that.

And . . .

And the fact that I don't have anything more to add is a sad story. I can't help feeling desperate that my life is so dull. To be honest, what makes me the most depressed these days is that nothing stands out about it. My life is so lacking in dimension, so shallow, that you couldn't plant a single mustard seed in it. Is it worth living like this?

I've begun to grow anxious about my insignificant life, and I'm twenty-five, ripe for marriage. There must be a connection there. Like a lot of women my age, I've got two men who might propose to me in the near future. It's a strange thing. When you're in your twenties, opportunities tied to "love" come knocking at your door. Even a girl like me, who doesn't have anything to be especially proud of, has her share of men who are interested. When you've got the youth of your twenties, you have an invincible weapon.

High school classmates of mine who have already gotten married can offer expert testimony about how to wield this weapon. I'm not going to name names, but take K, for example. She's chubby, talks non-stop, and, in addition, has a face that's impossible to read. But last year she married a young supermarket owner, who, from the look of things, is almost perfect. I don't have the slightest clue why he chose K. She said that they first met when she used to drop into his market to buy milk. Milk brought about this miracle. Milk . . .

M, a sickly friend of mine, had anemia. Even when we were still at school she would be absent for long stretches, just like that. I remember her mother in tears, saying, "I don't want my daughter to be sick in bed any more. The only thing I want is for her to be able to live on her own." But it's already two years since M married a handsome doctor. She said that he found her when she fainted in a hospital corridor. He transferred her to a room, and that was the beginning of love. This time it was anemia that brought about the miracle. Anemia . . .

Still, not everyone in their twenties, no matter how sparkling they are, has a dramatic tale of love to tell. Especially someone like me, unexcitable and sarcastic about everything. Even if a moment of drama came hunting for me, I'd probably kick it away and grumble about it afterwards: "I didn't expect this sort of childish stuff to happen."

So, of course, I was thoroughly blasé about the two men who've appeared in my life. There have been plenty of moments when I could've chosen to get all sugary, but I never acted upon them. Yes, I know it's a bit harsh to refuse to give into being sentimental or childish, but that's the way I've approached the world and I'm firm about it. That's also why I don't have many friends. I'm staunchly against sentimentality and childishness.

If you think about it, this attitude of mine could have had the same effect as K's milk and M's anemia. I truly believe that. When you're in your twenties all sorts of things can work miracles where love is concerned. That's the age to be swept away by something: love, work—as long as something captivates you, your life will suddenly be richer.

And that's where the problem lies. Light is dawning little by little. I can see that I was depressed yesterday, and the day before that too. Not depressed enough to shout out in desperate tears upon waking, but I've definitely been different from how I used to be. I thought about it all while I was walking, while I was working, and while I was sleeping. I thought about it when I saw blissful loving couples. I thought about it when I saw the co-worker at the desk next to mine—every day is a pleasure for her, because she loves hiking and spends her weekends in the mountains. I thought about it when I saw one of my classmates—she said over and over that she would be truly happy if she could do nothing but study until the day she died. Now she's gone to America as an exchange student.

But me? What can you say about me? A twenty-five-year-old who up to now has looked at life as a cynical spectator. A twenty-five-year-old who has never experienced the joy that comes from falling in love with anything. Someone who has never seriously tallied up the balance sheet of her life. Someone who is letting life slip through her fingers. Someone who is frittering away her precious youth chasing after a few measly won, all for the sake of piddling improvements in her impoverished life.

What's even worse is my grumbling that I could choose between two men and get married without ever falling in love. There's absolutely no reason I have to get married so quickly. The problem is that I don't see anything else ahead of me to add substance to my life. Letting myself be swept up in marriage is a way to fight my angst about my meager existence. If only I could guarantee that I wouldn't wind up making a dumb choice, then I could genuinely resolve to think everything through carefully.

Right. The way I've been living is just like the title of that old pop song: "Like A Fool." I realized this only very gradually. A growing awareness trickled into my mind, like water from a jar with a narrow crack. At first it leaked in drop by drop. Then the crack slowly grew bigger, until the realization gushed in and flooded my thoughts, and then, this morning, I could no longer restrain that desperate cry: "Enough! I can't go on living like this! I've got to make every second of my life count. That's exactly what I've got to do!"

But what power caused me to hold out until my mind was flooded like this? To let myself become so lethargic that I was finally overwhelmed by a shameful feeling that I was throwing my life away?

At last. Now I feel like I'm getting to the heart of the matter. Some sense of tension I can't quite put my finger on has been making me heap up all these useless words precisely to get to this point. My life has fallen into a rut because I must have wanted to have this morning's outburst. I need to justify my existence.

To say that I have to expose my mother's life in order to justify my own sounds really silly—maybe even shameful, coming as it does from a fully grown adult of twenty-five. I felt uncomfortable enough with the idea that I stopped sifting through all these issues long ago and buried them deep inside me. But I console myself that I can start this examination once more. I don't need to feel embarrassed just because I have to talk about my mom in groping after the roots of my own life.

My mother was born with an identical twin sister. They looked so similar that even their parents had a hard time telling them apart. My grandmother drilled this into my ears until I thought they would fall off. The two had identical features, personalities, grades, everything. Inseparable, clad in the same clothes and thinking the same thoughts in the same house, they seemed like a single person divided in two. Pulling the two of them apart was inconceivable.

My mother and my aunt finally became two individuals with their marriages. And as soon as they were split into two, their lives began to diverge so rapidly it seemed a god had decreed that one would receive all the bliss the world held and the other would receive all its misery. Unfortunately, my fate was to be born into this world on the side burdened with misery.

When I was young, I was deeply confused by my mother and my aunt. Who wouldn't have been, seeing my mother crying in a leaky shack and then witnessing my aunt, with the same face and the same voice, coming out of her bedroom wearing silk pyjamas? I felt like I was watching a play in which one actress played two roles, first performing as my weepy mother, and then running backstage to change into silk bedclothes and re-emerge as a different woman, a happy woman. At that point life's fatigue had not yet been fully etched into my mother's face and it was as difficult as ever to distinguish between the two.

To be honest, what probably made me so confused was my inability to accept that the woman in the silk pyjamas was not my mother. If I had been my aunt's daughter, would I have been as perplexed by my poor, rough aunt and my wealthy, gentle mother? In fact, my cousin, who is exactly my age, used to declare that she never once felt any confusion about the aunt who was her mother's twin. She always said with an aloof expression, "There's your mother . . ."

I stopped comparing "your mother"—that is, my mother—and my aunt at almost the same time I began to run away, because I had, as people say, "nothing to do." I couldn't grasp at all how two people who had started from the exact same point could turn out so differently, so I wound up losing curiosity about life. If it was fate, what could I do about it? In my adolescence I came to the conclusion that life was not something to inquire about, but something you had to accept. My mother's experience stole away my motivation to try to lead an exciting life.

It's really strange. Putting things in order like this is very depressing. It's really strange to take the thoughts floating vaguely in your mind, like seeds of grass scattering in the wind, and to meditate upon them. To arrange them until they wind up shocking you.

I definitely don't want to blame my mother for the chaos in my life. I don't particularly trust people who pin the responsibility for everything on family or society or the system. Sometimes I meet kids who try to justify their self-indulgence with these sorts of explanations, but I can't stand their rhetoric. Empty-headed fifteen- or sixteen-year-olds who parrot excuses like that are the worst. I can hardly keep myself from slapping them. Smart alecks without an ounce of self-respect.

So I want to talk about my unhappy mother and my happy aunt as objectively as I can. Even though the older generation's situation may be a delicate subject, it's not the only determining factor in my life.

And yet. And yet. What about the following quote? "We think others' unhappiness is natural. Our own unhappiness, though, we can never accept."

I discovered the passage accidentally in a book a while ago, and I think it's a real pearl of wisdom. To be honest, it's precisely this quote that gave me the courage to drag my mother into a defense of my life. That's how life is: in it "I," of course, had to be happy. The individual known as "I" has enormous value for me. When I realized that I didn't have to be ashamed of loving myself, a light bulb went on in my head.

Right. I can't go on living like this. I can see now how bumbling I've been with my own life. From now on I'm going to examine it carefully and not let it drift aimlessly. I'm going to turn it decisively in the right direction when the proper moment comes. Life is not something that is simply to be accepted. It's something to be lived in a spirit of adventure, even if that means risking it all.

That's what life is . . .

2 Lies

A life of poverty
Allows us nothing
Except a pose of desperation.

For some reason my bus didn't come. And while I was waiting for this bus that never came, a drop of rain suddenly landed on my forehead, followed, at one-second intervals, by drops on my cheek and on the bridge of my nose. I turned around to find shops with overhanging eaves and wasted no time taking refuge beneath them along with everyone else. Up to that point I hadn't done anything wrong.

But the shop whose eaves I was borrowing belonged to a florist, and in my pocket was the meager salary I had received from my boss only an hour before. Well, I can definitely get away with some roses, I thought . . . there was nothing to remind me that today was the first of April, that famous day, the day of fools. If I bought a bouquet of roses on payday, I figured, no harm would come to the world. So I bought the flowers. At 7:15 p.m., on the first of April, April Fool's Day. Of all days.

There was nothing wrong in what I did after that either. I had no way of knowing when my bus would arrive to take me home to Yeokchon-dong, the rain was gradually falling harder, and an empty taxi had miraculously stopped right in front of me. The driver got out, bought a pack of cigarettes at a store, and quickly got back in. If the taxi had just finished its errand and been on its way, nothing would have happened, but the driver slowly unwrapped the gold plastic stripe on the cigarette pack and, just as slowly and deliberately, tore the silver foil on the top to leave a square opening. He drew out a cigarette. Then he took a minute to look for his lighter. And another minute to light up and roll down his window. At last I opened the door and climbed into the back seat. There was still plenty left over from my meager salary in my pocket.

"Cheongdam-dong."

Right. I said Cheongdam-dong, not Yeokchon-dong. I know nobody asked me why I went to Cheongdam-dong, but I can't stand not explaining my own reasoning to myself. I looked at it this way. Taking a taxi to Yeokchon-dong, north of the river, would be a waste of money. Going to Cheongdam-dong made sense, though, since I could get there on the basic fare. Besides, wandering in the rain with a bouquet of red roses wouldn't be showing them proper respect.

Up until that point everything I did on the evening of April Fool's Day was accidental, as I've been explaining in detail. I was minding my own business, but fate kept pushing me in a particular direction—the bus, the rain, the roses, and finally the taxi driver, who put the finishing touch on this chain of coincidence. It all fit together as perfectly as if it had been measured out with a ruler. I'm not kidding, even if it was April Fool's Day. Actually, since it was April Fool's Day, all this was even more . . .

"No, please, don't kid me like that!"

That's what my grandfather cried out to the obstetrician on this day over fifty years ago, waving his hands wildly and practically shouting. His words have been handed down as a family joke for ages. As if that weren't enough, he added, "Don't tell me even doctors play gags on April Fool's Day."

At first Grandfather insisted the doctor's sober news that his wife had given birth to twin girls must be a joke. Even after seeing both daughters at the same time with his own eyes, disbelief remained on his face for quite a while. Because they were born on April Fool's Day, of all days, Grandfather somehow always doubted the event.

His suspicions were perfectly reasonable. After five years of marriage and no children, Grandmother had finally become pregnant, but her belly stuck out so little over the course of the next nine months that Grandfather was always suspicious about her pregnancy. So to learn that not one but two daughters had been in her womb . . . well, if it wasn't a silly April Fool's Day prank, then what was it? A sudden piece of good luck—or bad?

And on April 1st, twenty-five years later, Grandfather married off his two daughters at a wedding hall simultaneously. "They were given to me together, so I have to send them away together. I know it sounds crazy, but I'm marrying them off today."

My grandfather is thus remembered by his descendants for the singular act of tying the two most important dates in his twin daughters' lives to April 1st.

And today, once more, was April 1st.

On a whim, I found myself standing in front of my aunt's house in Cheongdam-dong. A bulb cast an elegant scarlet glow over the gate. I hesitated. Ordinarily I wouldn't drop in on the spur of the moment. My aunt was fond of me, but it took several phone calls on her part to drag me to visit. I never did anything like this.

Besides, there was no particular need for me to come today, when it was not only her birthday but her wedding anniversary. After all, my aunt and my mother's destinies were linked. A special occasion for one was just as special for the other.

But I was in Cheongdam-dong, not at home. I couldn't help it. At any rate, here I stood, and, besides, it would have been pointless to bring my mother flowers. That's the way things were at my house. Bring roses home? Forget it. A lifestyle in which roses were gifts was not something we were used to. A life of poverty allows us nothing but a pose of desperation.

My aunt was at home, but she was all dressed up. It was clear that she'd be heading out the door in five minutes.

"Mercy! Getting such a beautiful bouquet from you today. I'm going to treasure these flowers forever, until they turn to dust. Really. Just wait and see."

That's the sort of person Auntie was. Her way of expressing everything with certainty could suddenly wash away the ambiguous, complicated thoughts someone like me struggled with. She used vocabulary like "forever" and "treasure" at the drop of a hat, while my mother would utter terms like "profit" and "account" several times a day. But the one who had the profit and the bulging accounts throughout her life was definitely my aunt.

She set the bouquet above the fireplace and grabbed my hand. "Come on, let's go. I'd been planning to have a boring night out with your boring uncle. But now that you're here, Jin-jin, dinner will be deliriously delightful. You'll come along, won't you?"

Just as my aunt said, my uncle was truly boring. What she probably meant by "boring" was not that he was tiresome, but that every single thing about him was predictable. He never once forgot to celebrate their anniversary with dinner and a present, and he supported his family and his home with a solid earnestness. He did this all so naturally that he never felt a need to take credit for it. I certainly didn't have to worry that I'd hurt his feelings by butting in on their special dinner for my aunt's birthday and their anniversary. Somehow I couldn't refuse my Auntie's request, and I decided to do as she asked.

It had been ages since I'd been in a car my aunt was driving. When I was young, I used to be packed into her car and whisked off to her house frequently enough—whenever Mom was in crisis, the one sure SOS she had was to call my aunt. Auntie would come at any time without complaining and help my brother and me escape to her house. As soon as my father started his drunken ravings, my mother would phone her, and we'd hurry out the front gate and wait until she arrived. Did my aunt remember those days?

"Of course. Actually, it was thanks to you that I improved my driving so quickly. That's when I learned to go over the speed limit and to run red lights.

If it wasn't for your family, why would I ever have needed to get anywhere so fast? I even thought of buying a siren but Uncle was against it. It sure would have been fun to put one on the roof and race around, though."

My aunt looked as though she still regretted that she never got to do it. For my mother and me those memories were shameful, but to my aunt they were in part amusing reminiscences. But that wasn't the whole of it. She wasn't oblivious.

"Jin-jin, just forget about those times. Or try to think of it all as an interesting adventure story like I do. You can say that even though the world may be dull these days, back then it was really thrilling."

Is Auntie bored now? I suddenly turned to study her profile. She looked at least ten years younger than my mother. They might have been so similar when they were growing up that even their parents had trouble telling them apart, but now without being told no one would know that they were twins and not just sisters who looked a lot alike. My mother is the older sister, of course. Despite arriving into this world barely ten minutes before my aunt, a life of poverty has made her look as though she were born a full ten years earlier.

My aunt and uncle had settled upon a place that met their standards for dinner, an authentic French restaurant at a hotel. Auntie went into further detail for me. There wasn't anything she had been particularly keen on having and they had wavered a long time before making up their minds. If my family went out to eat—which, of course, didn't happen more than a few times a year—deciding where to go wasn't an issue; it was barbecued pork ribs, for sure. The restaurant we went to had a reputation for delicious food, and smoke from the roasting meat billowed all the way outside. Just as Mom bragged, every room was filled with people and even eating here meant work. You had to keep turning the meat, constantly shifting your seat to avoid the smoke. Then, once you wrapped your strips of pork in lettuce and popped them in your mouth, your cheeks felt as if they would burst and you had to chew ferociously. My mother, brother and I would use every ounce of strength we had, struggling with the pork, like soldiers in battle. And when the battle was over, we would file out of the restaurant in exhausted silence.

My aunt and uncle's dining experience could hardly have been more different. A waiter, smelling pleasantly of cologne, guided them to the place they had reserved, as sweet notes from a piano, seemingly live, drifted among the tables occupied by elegant couples. I don't feel like going on about the refined settings with their spotless tablecloths or the napkins folded to look like flowers. And I won't talk about my uncle's precise arrival, the practiced way he ordered, and the picture-perfect dishes that appeared one course at a time. I've gotten too old to be intimidated by stuff like that. Besides, I still had plenty left over from my meager salary to pay for that dinner. I just didn't want to.

Instead, I have a few things to say about my uncle, or rather, the scene created by my aunt and uncle. My uncle showed up at the exact time they had arranged. He limited the wine he drank to a glass or two. Of course he stays away from cigarettes—bad for your health. Every morning he works out for an hour without fail—essential for a middle-aged man. My flawless uncle, like the flawless uncle he is, came prepared with a small jewelry box as an anniversary and birthday gift.

Lovingly, he said, "Black pearls like these are considered precious all over the world. I was going to buy you a matching necklace but I'll save the rest for next year. So here's a ring. I hope you like it."

"Thank you. Of course I like it. I like anything you pick." My aunt's response came out as smoothly as if it had been scripted.

"How many anniversaries have we celebrated without the kids now?" My uncle clinked his wineglass against his wife's. He was talking about their children Ju-ri and Ju-hyeok, whom they'd sent overseas to study.

"Almost ten years. But today we've got Jin-jin with us." My aunt, becoming more concerned about me than my uncle, dragged me into the conversation.

"Indeed. And are things going well at the company?" My uncle scarcely turned his attention toward me.

"Yes. Mom's going to be eternally grateful you helped me find a good position."

I misrepresented my mother's reaction. In fact, she had snorted, "What? You mean he can think about somebody beside his own wife and kids?"

"I had this wine set aside especially for you when I made the reservation. Let's have another glass," said my uncle, focusing his interest on my aunt once more.

"Jin-jin brought me some roses. Isn't she thoughtful, worrying I'm lonely with our kids so far away?" Auntie struggled to bring me back into the conversation I'd been elbowed out of.

"Thank you."

My uncle, with his traditional manners. He knew how to go about the formalities of etiquette in the most formal way. At that moment I caught my aunt burying her lips in her wineglass and sighing softly. We weren't even halfway through the meal and just as she had predicted, I was really getting bored. My aunt looked bored too. The only one who wasn't bored was my boring uncle.

Uncle runs a very well-known architecture firm that specializes in office buildings. They say he has an amazing talent for creating economical and practical space, which means he's constantly gaining contracts. But even with this endless supply of jobs, he doesn't need to work to the point of neglecting his family. According to my aunt, he just consults with clients and dreams up the basic layout; some ten employees take care of the rest. When I think about Uncle, with his fair complexion, leaving for work in a stylish suit and ending the day on schedule, the title "architect" that is stamped on his name card somehow doesn't fit. I've never found in him a trace of dust or shouts to workers or reinforced steel or concrete. Still, he is definitely an architect. A pretty boring one.

Every so often during the course of our tedious dinner, I scanned the tables around us. I couldn't get over the peaceful atmosphere that reigned everywhere. No differences of opinions, no raised voices, no hurled liquor glasses, not even a tossed napkin. Instead it was soft piano music, soft conversation and soft-voiced waiters responding to the diners. For a moment I had the illusion that I was sitting in some enormous, well-tended aquarium and lost my appetite for the meat I was chewing.

At the pork rib restaurant, chaos ruled. You could always count on a fight breaking out among at least one group of customers, followed by flung liquor bottles and smashed plates. You had to shout at the top of your lungs to order more. It may have been a battlefield, but it wasn't boring. How can anyone be bored when bombs are exploding and bullets are whizzing past?

"The ice cream here is really delicious. Don't you think so, honey?"

Uncle was tucking into his dessert with gusto. Being used to ice cream bars from the mom-and-pop stores in my neighborhood, I wasn't especially taken with it, but I kept quiet. It was my aunt's agreement he was after.

"Yes. It's very tasty." My aunt always answered my uncle's questions instantly as if she had been waiting for them. And always with the answer he wanted. "Shall we order more?"

With equal promptness Uncle gave the proper answer to Auntie's suggestion. "No thanks. More than one scoop wouldn't be healthy."

My aunt appeared briefly rattled by his response. I know she doesn't like such perfect answers. She set her spoon down in the ice cream dish and seemed to stifle a sigh.

Just then, I remembered something that happened when I was in fifth grade. In junior high I developed a reputation as a problem child, but back in elementary school I was a model student. Shortly before Teacher's Day, in May of that year, something came up that caused me a lot of anguish. As one of the day's special activities, my teacher wanted to ask my mother to be among the guest instructors. The root of the problem? I had written "businesswoman" as her occupation on the form about my family background. In fact, at the time Mom was hawking cheap socks in a market.

Each class had two parents designated "Teacher for the Day." The other person chosen for our class was my friend's father, a well-known professor at a top university. It was crazy. I chased my teacher up to the faculty room and made several weak excuses, but she said no other parents were suitable and that she'd call my mother directly. My teacher calling my mother? Being as young as I was, I gasped and croaked out right away, "No, don't worry. I'll make sure she comes! I promise!"

And so, in May of that year, on Teacher's Day, one of those designated to lead a special lesson for Grade 5, Class 3, was the mother of An Jin-jin. Me. When she entered, wearing a stylish, light grey two-piece suit, elegantly made up and coiffured, the kids roared with a single voice. "Wow!"

It was the sort of exclamation that would greet a beautiful young student teacher. That's how much of a hit the mother of An Jin-jin was. My mother.

I have a confession to make. My classmates never knew, but the mother of mine who was such a hit in May of that year was not my mother. It was my aunt. After racking my brain, my mother's twin sister came to mind, and she was absolutely delighted at the thought of playing An Jin-jin's mother for a day. On that day, while Auntie was performing the dual roles of mother and teacher at school, Mom was selling socks in the market, completely in the dark about what was going on. The night before, she had wrapped two pairs of socks apiece for my brother and me to give to our homeroom teachers as presents. That was the best she could do. But I should make another confession. I didn't even give those socks to my teacher. Instead Auntie gave the teacher a crystal vase. I still remember what she said.

"I bought it because I thought they would go beautifully with a bouquet of purple lilacs. I do hope you'll accept it."

Where did she learn to speak like that? My mother wouldn't have bought a crystal vase, and even if she had, I thought, she certainly wouldn't have had said anything about the flowers she imagined in it. And so, in May of that year, my aunt went home, having allowed me to save face brilliantly. It goes without saying that from the next day on I walked with my head held high.

I can't be sure if my aunt still remembers what happened. We have never spoken about it. I took to avoiding her because I wanted her to forget about it as quickly as possible. I dreaded my mother finding out—not so much because I worried she might be hurt as because I couldn't come up with a good excuse for what I'd done. I didn't want to commit the foolish crime of stabbing her with the dagger of truth. I didn't want to sob, "I was wrong. I'm a horrible daughter. I felt ashamed of you."

While I was recalling what happened that May, Uncle had cleaned his ice cream dish and was now dabbing his lips with his napkin. My aunt, her head bowed, was still toying with her melting ice cream. I once heard someone say that marriage is like a dinner party where the soup is better than the dessert. Frivolously, I thought about it as I sat next to this couple who were celebrating their twenty-seventh wedding anniversary.

Looking up, I noticed a man standing next to the cash register. I had been under the impression that only elegant couples ate at this restaurant, but seeing him, I thought cattily, "So guys like him come here too." His long hair was disheveled, and he was wearing a baggy sweater and cotton pants that could not hide their wrinkles, despite their fashionable cut. Suddenly, though, I was so startled I almost shrieked.

He ran his hand through his hair and turned vacantly in my direction. Oh my god. It was definitely Kim Jang-u. At the very same moment he also seemed to realize it was definitely me. His eyes went wide and, grinning broadly, he lifted his right hand high in the air, like he usually did. Then he brought it down to his chest, as if to ask whether he should come to me, or whether I'd go to him for a little while. There was no time. He could come over at any moment.

"Excuse me a second." I went quickly towards him, not even noticing that my napkin had fallen to the floor.

"What in the world are you doing here?"

"What in the world are you doing here?"

Our questions came at almost the same time. Why the astonishment? Why should we be so flabbergasted by meeting in a French restaurant in a fancy hotel?

"I'm just as surprised to be here. I've been called into emergency action as a guide. Jang-ho paged me and asked if I'd take a client of his to somewhere in Yongsan, so I hurried over. He's been living in Paris and just came back to Korea yesterday for the first time in twenty years."

Kim Jang-u gestured with his eyes towards a middle-aged gentleman who was waiting a few steps ahead of him. The grey trench coat he was wearing seemed foreign. Kim Jang-u's brother ran a small travel agency, and occasionally he had to help him out at short notice. Now it was my turn to explain myself.

"That's your mother, isn't it? I can see it in her face."

No, it's my aunt. That's what I thought I was going to say, I swear that's what I thought I was going to say. But the words that came from my lips in reply—very naturally, without a moment's hesitation—were the following:

"It's my mom and my uncle. She owes him a special treat for dinner. Hey, you'd better go. Your guest is waiting."

"Okay. I'll introduce myself properly later. I'll give you a call. So long."

He gave my far-off aunt one more meaningful look and went over to the man wearing the grey trench coat. My aunt, puzzled, was sitting upright in her chair and sending penetrating looks our way. The man in the sweater whom she was scrutinizing so carefully? He happens to be one of the two men I'm thinking of marrying.

And suddenly—before I even knew what I was doing—I had tossed out the exact same lie I had made in fifth grade, but this time to a man I might marry. At 9:20 p.m. on April 1, that famous day, the day of fools.

This lie . . .

3 A Human Landscape

*M*y father's life belongs to my father.
 My mother's life belongs to my mother.
 I never once asked her
 Why she lives as she does.
 Even though she is my mother
 That would surely be a rude question.

A beautiful May evening. Yesterday's rain cleared the sky, letting the stars gleam again at long last, and the lilac scent that wafted from a distance, neither too overpowering nor too faint, made it all that much more atmospheric.

In my neighborhood small houses are jammed up against each other, with walls enclosing courtyards no bigger than the palm of your hand. Strangely enough, however, lilac bushes abound. When their branches are bare they are scarcely noticeable, but in late spring their lacy purple blossoms, together with their scent, brighten our shabby alleyway. At my house, though, there isn't a single bush.

My aunt had spoken of lilacs as she handed over the crystal vase, but her garden doesn't have lilacs either. And it isn't just her garden. A glance over the walls will confirm how rich the houses in her neighborhood are, but lilacs are uncommon. Despite their elegance, their scent, and the beauty of the name "lilac," the rich don't choose lilacs for their gardens. Instead they survive in the minuscule courtyards of the poor. I've been paying attention to lilacs every spring since I was in fifth grade, and I've even thought that if I were a plant, I'd want to be a lilac bush. But, at the risk of repeating myself, we don't have any lilacs at our house.

If I put it that way, somebody might well ask, "Then what kind of trees do you have?" None. No, actually, it's not that we don't have any trees, it's that we don't have a courtyard. Our house is built on twenty-seven *pyeong*[1] of land and it takes up eighteen of them. It's the smallest house around. After moving constantly within the neighborhood for more than ten years, we finally settled here three months ago—the first house my mother has owned in her twenty-seven years of marriage.

---

1. One *pyeong* is roughly equivalent to 3.3 square meters.

"So you've managed exactly one *pyeong* a year, Mom. No more, no less."

That's the calculation my brother Jin-mo made after comparing the amount of land she had and the number of years she had been married. My mother was too caught up in her happiness to notice his sarcasm. Instead she joined in cheerfully.

"Then, even if I don't lift a finger, in ten years I'll have ten more *pyeong* and in twenty years, there'll be twenty more. Our suffering is over now."

I think this was her way of saying that life has both ups and downs. Who can compete with Mom when it comes to subtraction? She sold socks, she sold underwear, and later she even sold towels, but she hardly ever had any money left over in her pockets. Her husband, her son, and the cruel world itself siphoned it away from her. Of course, I took some too.

The house is terribly small, but now, for the very first time, Jin-mo and I each have rooms genuinely worthy of the name. Jin-mo's bedroom is on the right as you enter, followed by mine to the left and then Mom's. The bathroom lies between my room and Jin-mo's, and the kitchen between mine and Mom's. In the back there's an extension for a long storeroom, and in front we've got a water tap we can use to our hearts' content. The only thing missing is a lilac bush.

If someone were to come in at this moment and look around, this is what he would find: light, darkness, light, darkness, light. Darkness from the bathroom and the kitchen, light from each of our three bedrooms. We've always been this way—people who have forgotten it's possible to leave two rooms empty in order to gather in one and liven up the atmosphere.

Still, Mom has been really happy these days, because, for whatever reason, Jin-mo doesn't come home late every night. Just seeing his light on cheers her up. That's probably also why the refrigerator has held a constant supply of hairtail, a type of fish that Jin-mo likes. I can't stand it. I don't think Mom can either, because my father was keen on the fish. But Jin-mo takes after him, so she buys it anyway.

Just say the word "hairtail," and my mood turns foul. The scent of lilacs becomes mingled with their fishy odor. Unable to bear it, I fling open my window. Well, I try to fling it open, but since my room is in the middle, the window is little more than a hole towards the back. I look vacantly out at the wall behind our house, my chin propped up in my hands. I can hear Jin-mo speaking in low tones through his own open window.

"Yeah. Uh huh . . . Over there? Okay. Then have those guys clear off . . . No, you don't have to. Send them all . . . Okay."

Seriously, I can't help bursting into laughter whenever I hear Jin-mo talking like that, no matter how hard I try not to. Right now I bet he's pressing his chin against his neck, trying to make his voice as low as possible, and concentrating all his energy into the lower part of his belly. Jin-mo is totally convinced that a voice dripping with authority and an expression to match are prerequisites for a gang leader. Once, through an open window, I saw Jin-mo, intense, practicing his low voice and gazing steely-eyed into a mirror.

"I already told you. The bigger it is, the more important it is to keep it under wraps. I won't tolerate any mistakes. Uh huh . . . Yeah. Be sure to keep those guys under control. Okay, enough!" I hear him put down the receiver, followed by a dry cough. After a minute of clearing his throat, he starts dialing again. Beep beep beep. I strain my ears, trying the whole time not to burst out laughing. Jin-mo lowers his voice once more.

"It's me. Yeah. Sorry I couldn't get there. Something came up. Yes, I'll give you another call, so wait . . . Good night. Okay. I do, too. Good night." Even though his tone is low, I can tell he's talking to a girl from an underlying sweetness in his voice. A girl . . . I think about his ex-girlfriends. Even before he joined the army, women had caused him several headaches. He got off to a brilliant start. In his first year of high school, his moustache just sprouting, he had already stirred up enough trouble with a girl to almost get himself expelled. Then (twice) there were the mothers who flew into our house and turned everything upside-down with tantrums; the so-called 'older brother' who came and threw Jin-mo to the floor when he was in the middle of dinner; and a senseless girl who hassled Mom by chasing her all the way to the market, asking to be accepted as a daughter-in-law. Even if I just keep to the major incidents, that's five right there. All this before he joined the army.

But Jin-mo rejected all those girls and did his military service. He's been leading a quiet life for almost a year now since being discharged. His only concern is his gang—putting it back together, keeping it running, managing it.

When I asked him why he's so busy that he's always running around and, at most, using the house to drop his laundry off, he answered, "Everything's screwed up. It became a complete mess while I was gone. There are a bunch of guys I've got to take care of, not just one or two. Do you think just anybody can lead a gang?"

My god, a gang? Jin-mo, a gang leader?

Like Mom, I thought some time in the army would straighten Jin-mo out, but now he's been spending all his time with his "organization" in an "organized" way. Even before he joined the army, he hung around with other troublemakers his own age, all of them broke. They'd get drunk and start brawls. Sometimes they'd even get themselves tossed into police holding cells. He was a constant headache to my mother. And now, three years later, not a single thing has changed.

I take that back. Everything is not the same. For one thing he has begun to speak in low tones. That's a major change. Jin-mo now looks like he's made up his mind to rise in this world, from petty troublemaker to gang leader. I suppose you could say he's done well for himself by rising above the status of local thug at his age. Let me put a positive spin on it: being a gang boss is a hundred times better for my only brother than being content to roam the streets at night as someone else's underling.

The problem, though, as I see it, is that his "organization" is really shoddy. The gang members who occasionally come and go at our house consist of three or four pimply-faced boys who were kicked out of high school, along with a few puny, wishy-washy cronies who'd never survive a fistfight in the first place. Jin-mo may be constantly going on about his organization this and his organization that, but it looks really pathetic to me.

Nonetheless, Jin-mo puts real effort into playing the part of gang boss, especially getting the look right—jet black suit, crisply pressed shirt, necktie, gleaming shoes, and hair that takes an hour to mousse back properly. Completely oblivious to what's going on, the boss's mother spends more than an hour every night ironing his shirt and trousers.

But Jin-mo's efforts to become a gang boss don't end there—active study is required, so he pursues his education with videos. He chain-smokes his way through *The Godfather* and *Hourglass*, watching Marlon Brando and Choe Min-su until his eyes get tired.[2] These two videos serve as his textbooks on the proper way for a gang boss to act. If Marlon Brando and Choe Min-su hadn't spoken in low tones, then neither would Jin-mo. If Marlon Brando hadn't enjoyed wearing black suits, my mother wouldn't have to spend every night doubled over an ironing board working on her son's shirt and trousers until her back aches.

But a girl . . .

I turned my focus to Jin-mo's new girlfriend again. As far as I can tell, he sees having a girlfriend as part of being a gang boss. For some time he has been devoting all his energy to maintaining both the gang and his prestige as a boss. If he has a new girlfriend, then she is not just a "woman" but "the boss's woman." She's not just another in the string of girlfriends he had before, back when it was easy come, easy go.

No, no.

I suddenly shook my head. It wasn't being boss, but the girl that came first. In other words, I may have events in the wrong order. The girl came along, and as a result Jin-mo wanted to become a boss. That's the sort of

---

2. *Hourglass* (*Moraeshigye*) was a popular SBS TV miniseries in the mid-'90s that featured the actor Choe Min-su as a member of the underworld.

person he is. Marlon Brando and Choe Min-su had appeared so that he could seem perfect for her. So what kind of a woman was she? In the old days my thoughts would probably have stopped at this point. After all, it's Jin-mo's life. Everyone knows how to lead a moral life. We have it driven into our heads in books and classes from elementary school on. Whether you go to school or not, you're bombarded with advice. Newspapers, magazines, books, radio, television—even today celebrities appear by the dozen and spout moving and proper words. Anyone who claims not to know is lying.

So everything was up to Jin-mo. It was none of my business. If he were still too young to understand the difference between right and wrong, then it would be my duty as an older sister to help look after him. I used to fulfill that duty conscientiously, and I'm proud of it. Our father had ruined us. To get us on our feet again and to support us, Mom had to leave for work at dawn, and so I would carry Jin-mo on my back, no questions asked. Sometimes I even went to school with him riding piggyback. It wasn't the 1950s, but that's how I spent my childhood.

I minded my own business throughout his adolescence, when he was as much a problem child as I was—no, much more of a problem. Then, it seemed to me that Jin-mo's life was his, just as my own belonged to me.

What a simple, obvious formula to live by. Likewise, my father's life belongs to my father. My mother's life belongs to my mother. I never once asked my mother why she lives as she does. Even though she is my mother, that would surely be a rude question. I've never put up with meddling like that from anyone else. If anyone said something like that to me, that was it. I'd never see them again. My wounded pride wouldn't let me forgive them.

People in families like ours had no right to talk about others, and my friends could confirm on the spot that I was famous for never giving my own opinion as advice. The people who annoy me most are the ones who rattle on with hackneyed expressions. I wanted words that were exceptional. People who kept their mouths shut when they didn't have anything particular to say, on the other hand, were no problem.

I can see now, though, that this approach to the world has several problems. Well, it's not that there have to be, but there might be. My life is my own, but as far as Jin-mo is concerned, it's also his sister's life, and for my mother, it's her daughter's life. Putting it in these terms, Jin-mo's life is my brother's, and once something has personal significance, it has a completely different level of importance. I can't just shut my mouth and stand idly by. In order to fully understand my own life, sometimes I have to look at my brother's, whether doing so makes a big difference to him or not.

So, in order to satisfy my curiosity about Jin-mo's woman—I mean, the boss's woman—I knocked on his door. Sure enough, he was leaning against the wall, his back propped up by a pillow, engrossed in studying. His expression was extremely serious. A sidelong glance confirmed today's textbook: *The Godfather*.

"What is it?" His tone was dignified.

At first he didn't use his boss's voice at home, but now it's become a habit—the influence of Marlon Brando and Al Pacino, for sure.

"Do you have a girlfriend again?"

Damn. I immediately regretted what I said. Even though my usual style is abrupt and I don't add much in the way of filler, saying "again" was a definite blunder. This time she was the boss's girlfriend . . .

And, sure enough, a frown appeared on Jin-mo's brow. Foreheads stand out prominently on people with slicked back hair. They reflect every emotion. His eyebrows remained knitted for a while and then he took out a cigarette. I glanced at the screen furtively. Just as expected. Marlon Brando was staring out the window, frowning and smoking a cigar.

"Yeah."

His gentle answer surprised me. A pause, and a cool-headed response that masks emotion? *The Godfather* for sure.

"A good kid," Jin-mo added tersely, blowing smoke into the air.

"We don't have to worry this time?"

My question was elliptical. What I was really saying was, given the past, Mom and I can't help being nervous if you've met a girl; do we have to stay on alert this time too and keep our eye on how it all develops?

"You haven't changed a bit, sis," Jin-mo snorted. He pressed "stop" on the VCR, and the image of Al Pacino standing stiffly in front of his father faded to black. Jin-mo puffed wordlessly on his cigarette for a while, then asked, "Have you ever had a lover?"

A lover? I've always felt that people who used the term "lover" were shallow. But I couldn't react to every single word of Jin-mo's. That would be about as silly as asking a crow why it was a crow. And, in fact, if he had asked me if I had ever been in love, I'd have felt nauseous. That would have been much worse. Sometimes shallowness can be as refreshing as the feeling of cotton cloth on your skin.

I cut him off coldly. "*You* talk. And stop being such a smart aleck." I'm not one to sit and share words like "lover" or "in love" calmly with anybody, let alone my cheeky little brother.

"Want a drink?"

Huh? Jin-mo pulled out a bottle of liquor from under his desk. I took a closer look. It wasn't *soju*,[3] but whiskey. Jin-mo swigged a shot from the bottle, frowned, and wiped his lips. He looked as though he'd been practicing a while. I had a gulp from the bottle myself, although I couldn't do it with Jin-mo's panache, of course.

"Smells nice, huh? Good liquor makes me want to have a good woman around."

That was Jin-mo. If he were capable of saying, "Good liquor makes me want good friends around" instead, well, that wouldn't be him. My suspicion that the woman showed up before his becoming boss was almost certainly correct. I had another shot and passed the bottle back to him. This time I swallowed a bit more. I felt a fire in my throat and then alcohol spreading in my gut. A little more, and my whole body would grow warm and I'd feel fine. I like hard liquor because of this feeling. I don't want to brag that I'm a good drinker, but I know how to enjoy booze. If Jin-mo and I inherited anything in common, it's an affinity for alcohol.

"I decided something during my three years in the army. I wanted to make something of myself. When I got out, I wanted to have at least one thing in my life that worked out. That's what I decided. It's really unfair. When guys get crew cuts and put on those baggy uniforms, they're all zeroes. So how come some of them have so much? Bastards. One guy was from Seoul National—read English like it was nothing. Another one said his dad is a millionaire. Didn't bat an eyelash. What's worse, their girlfriends come to visit them and they all look like TV stars. Where did they find babes like that? I felt like my own life was worthless. So . . ."

He paused to take a swig from the bottle.

"So this time you found yourself a decent girl?"

"I tried . . ." He stroked his hair all the way back and flashed a satisfied grin. Suddenly he became serious. "Come close and listen." He was being childish, but because he was my younger brother—or maybe because of the alcohol—I humored him. When I leaned over, he whispered a name slowly and distinctly into my ear and then studied my face for a reaction.

"Do you recognize the name?"

Of course I did. But I had no idea why it had tumbled from Jin-mo's lips and shook my head. The name was one anyone would recognize; it belonged to the head of a *chaebol*, a business conglomerate. But there are plenty of

---

3. The most popular distilled liquor in Korea.

people around who have the same names and I didn't show any reaction. Jin-mo, though, became animated.
"Don't be surprised. That's who it is. That's exactly who it is!"
"What are you talking about?" I got the feeling that this wasn't a joke. My interest was suddenly piqued. On the other hand, as before, I had tended to have lots of doubts about this brother of mine and asked the question with an attitude of indifference.
"I was stunned at first too. She's really sweet. A dove, she's just like a dove. No. That's not quite right. She's like a dove shivering in a cold rain. I've never met anyone like her before." Jin-mo strung his answer out slowly for effect.
"Your dove's father runs a *chaebol*?" I cut to the point—I don't like word games.
"Sort of."
"Sort of?"
"This is just between you and me. Even my gang doesn't know. She's a very close relative."

Just as I thought. I was a little disappointed and even more disappointed at my own disappointment. But Jin-mo remained exultant.
"He's her uncle. Isn't that amazing? It's incredible. At first I thought she was lying, but I had some of my kids do a little investigating and it's true. Her dad's name is on the list of relatives for all the holiday gatherings at his house."
"You're pathetic. On the list of relatives for holiday gatherings? That's really special. Amazingly special."
I was being sarcastic, but I felt lonely all of a sudden. The moment the phrase "list of relatives for holiday gatherings" came out of my own mouth, an overwhelming loneliness made me bitter. Hadn't I always tried not to interfere in other people's lives precisely to avoid this feeling? But it was already too late. Since I had gone this far, I decided to add more. After all, this was the question that had led me to knock on Jin-mo's door in the first place.
"So this time Mom and I won't have to suffer because of your girl troubles. Well, of course. Our Jin-mo wouldn't just dump a girl who's like a dove—I mean, a girl who's on the list of relatives of a *chaebol* chairman?"
Suddenly Jin-mo's expression became serious, and he stared at me for a long moment. Then, looking off into space, he gave an affected laugh. This string of actions was certainly cribbed from Choe Min-su, but now it came naturally to him. Practice is a very frightening thing, I thought idly.
Solemnly, he said, "Love . . . love. No matter how you try not to fall in love, it doesn't work that way. And even if you want to have a love that lasts forever, things don't go the way you planned. Do you know what I mean?"

He had given a lot of thought to his declaration. His words were intended to be a piece of art that would emphasize two things in profound, stylish packaging: he was asking me a) to acknowledge that it wasn't because she came from a rich family that he had decided to fall in love, and b) not to inquire about his responsibility for what might happen in the future. His complicated love life couldn't have amounted to absolutely nothing so far. Considering all the effort Jin-mo had put into his relationships, there was nothing remarkable in his words.

I felt like I had learned everything I wanted to, but even so, there was no reason to think Jin-mo's dealings with women would be the slightest bit different this time. If the result of our conversation was simply that Jin-mo and I reconfirmed our sense of each other, that was enough. No. There was one more thing—the beauty of a brother and sister sitting together and having a drink on a spring evening amidst the faint scent of lilacs.

As soon as I made a motion to leave, Jin-mo picked up the remote and hit "play." Al Pacino reappeared and there was the sound of gunfire. I was about to close the door but then whirled around.

"It's a little strange to call your sweetheart a delicate little dove. I mean, the guy she likes is watching gangster movies over and over because of her."

Jin-mo blinked twice before he understood what I was saying. Then he grinned, bewildered, unable to hide his astonishment at being found out. Dropping his guard for a moment, Jin-mo pushed aside Al Pacino and Choe Min-su, and his own natural expression reappeared. The look on his face closely resembled Dad's look when he sobered up and surveyed the mess he had created in our house.

"Hmm. There's some truth in that. Maybe I should call her a fearless dove—she said that to her, the coolest guys in the world are gang leaders. Yeah, these days women are all like that. They go wild over gang stories. Look at the big hits now. They're all about organized crime. Guys in gangs are idols."

Gang. Gang. The word gave Jin-mo a thrill.[4] It hadn't occurred to me that it wasn't just a lone dove, but the word itself that was pushing Jin-mo into organized crime. When did all this happen? At some point when I wasn't paying attention, the world had snuck up and . . .

I left Jin-mo. He looked as though he could spend hours sitting there as long as he could glean some information about life as a gangster. As I entered my room, though, something strange happened. I felt like I had unknowingly

---

4. We omit a line that uses offers an etymological explanation impossible to capture in English: the word used for "gang" in the Korean text is *jopok*. Jin-jin goes on to say, "I knew that the word *jopok* was a short way of saying organized band of thugs (*jojik pongnyeokbae*), but . . ."

been infected. Gang, gang, gang. The sound kept reverberating in my head. But when I pricked up my ears, I realized there was something bubbling over in the kitchen, going bang bang bang.[5]

A chicken was boiling. The light in my mother's room was still on. She must have been about to go and finish preparing it, but I decided to sneak a glance into her room as I passed by. It wouldn't be a bad idea to spend time with her until the chicken was done. Assuming that she would welcome my visit, that is.

I called her quietly from outside her room, but there was no answer. I opened the door only to find her lying asleep without any covers, using her arms as a pillow. Her account book lay right next to her head. She had probably set her aching back down on the floor after calculating how many panties and T-shirts she had sold, how many pairs of socks she had handed over to customers, how much profit she had made, how much more she would need to sell to pay her contribution to her rotating credit club. And the chicken?

I was going to put a pillow under her head, lay a blanket on her gently so as not to disturb her with the movement of the air, and leave the room quietly. I could put out the blue gas flames heating the pot of chicken. I'd done plenty of cooking for myself ever since the ripe age of ten. On days when I was feeling like a particularly good girl, I'd make bean paste stew, prepare vegetables, get the dinner table ready and wait for Mom to come home from the market. But once I turned fifteen the days I felt like a good girl were few and far between. It was strange. You're supposed to become nicer as you mature, but that wasn't the case with me. As I grew older and looked around more, it seemed that all the nice kids I knew were idiots. And at the time I just didn't want to be a fool.

Everything was fine until I put a blanket over her. As soon as I tried to prop her head up with a pillow, she jumped out of bed and cried out, as if she'd only been pretending to be asleep all along.

"What? What's going on?"

My mother looked around the room, her face blanched with fear, true to form. Unless her eyes open of their own free will, she always cries out, startled. It doesn't matter if it's morning, noon or the middle of the night: What? What's going on?

"For god's sake, calm down. It's just me." Only then did she relax. Stroking her slightly swollen face, she glanced at her watch.

---

5. The boiling sound here in Korean is represented by the onomatopoetic *pok, pok, pok*; (cf. "gang," *jopok*).

"What are you boiling a chicken for?" Somehow I couldn't hold back my irritation when I saw her like this.

"Did you turn the gas off?"

"It's boiling right now. I just asked why you're cooking a chicken."

"I put it on for Jin-mo a little while ago. I must have dozed off while I was lying down."

My mother had calmed down, but she became as animated as if she'd never been asleep, folding up the blanket and pushing the pillow aside. She spoke as though she was spoiling for a fight. It's an amazing talent she has, of springing to life like a toy dog that's been wound up. It always stuns me, even though I'm as quick to react as she is. At first I'm annoyed when I see her as exhausted and limp as bits of straw, but then I grow even more hostile when she becomes wound up again.

"Don't you have anything to do? I don't feel like sleeping anymore." She lifted a book from underneath her ledger.

"What's that?"

I did my best to control my growing irritation and managed to scrape up some interest in her affairs. Blocking the cover of the book with her hand, she motioned with her eyes for me to hurry up and get out.

"What book is that?"

Now my curiosity was piqued. If Mom was reading, it meant something serious was up, and the book's contents would furnish the main clue as to what. On those few occasions when she faces problems that are beyond her, she rushes to a neighborhood bookstore as a last resort and chooses a book that offers a solution. She's like a student preparing for exams who wrestles for a while with a difficult math problem before suddenly remembering the answer key at the back of the book.

As far as I can remember, the person who gave Mom the most trouble was my father. She read several thick books because of him. In the end, though, she discovered that answers don't lie in books, and she has hardly done any reading since. The only books I can think of that she's read lately are an autobiography by some successful businesswoman, a lively text by an education professor about dealing with problem kids, and— when she heard there was money to be had in raising mudfish—a book entitled *Raising Mudfish*. But these books, which she had to fight off drowsiness to get through, were no help. She did not become a successful businesswoman. Jin-mo and I did not grow up to be children she could be proud of. The mudfish? She didn't have any capital—she couldn't even make a start.

My aunt liked books too, but she never read the books my mother read and vice-versa. The last time I saw her, she asked if I knew the story about the photographer who took pictures of bridges.[6] When I mention the title of a novel, she'll say, "Oh, that one" and she'll relate her impressions of it to me for a long time. And what else was it she said? Oh yeah. These days she's learning a song by Yang Hui-eun: "Love, and its Loneliness." I think she even mentioned that she burnt a pot of strawberry jam she was boiling down while she was singing the song over and over at the piano.

"Are you reading a novel too?" If Auntie can do it, so can Mom. It's possible for her to change as she gets older. Ignoring her scowl, I practically tore the book away from her hands.

"What's this? First . . . Steps . . . In . . . Japanese? 'This perpetual bestseller that teaches Japanese conversation has sold over a million copies.'"

"Yes, your mother has decided to learn some Japanese. So what?"

No novel this time either.

"I'm going to give up selling underwear. There's no money in it. Lots of Japanese come to the market these days, so I'm thinking about selling the stuff they like. It doesn't matter how much underwear I sell—I'm just not making money. Nowadays only hicks wear what I have for sale. Younger people turn their noses up at it. You know what they tell me? 'Underwear should be stylish too.' I have nothing I can say to that."

"What do the Japanese want?"

"Ginseng, seaweed, kimchi, vegetables pickled in soy sauce. They're really on the lookout for that sort of stuff. They buy it up by the boxload. These days the shops that do best only deal with Japanese, but I can't speak the language. I'm going to work through this book and then figure out what to do. All I need to do is get started and I'll be okay."

She laughed cheerfully, as if brimming with confidence. Her laugh gets livelier with each passing day. If there's one thing about my mother worth looking into, it's her incredible vitality. By all rights she shouldn't have any, but she has the power to constantly recreate this energy and invest it back into her life. And this power of hers keeps getting stronger as she grows older. The sighs and laments from when she was younger have disappeared, and all that's left in their wake is an incomprehensible tenacity. Every day she dies and is reborn.

The mysterious energy my mother has is the secret of life, and it's something else I've got to think about carefully in the future. If I investigate her, analyze her, then I just might figure out the right words to express what her endless energy is all about.

---

6. Yang Gui-ja is referring here to *The Bridges of Madison County* by Robert James Waller.

My fifty-two-year-old mother grasps *First Steps in Japanese* and laughs. My fifty-two-year old aunt says seriously that she's learning "Love, and its Loneliness." For the first time it occurred to me that the two of them really are twins for reasons beyond their similar looks. They are similar, but then again they are not utterly identical. How are they alike? How are they different?

"Go off to bed. I'm going to learn this damn *hiragana* and then get some sleep.[7] Oh, turn the gas off on your way. The chicken should be done by now. Give it to Jin-mo in the morning. I don't want you sleeping late just because it's Sunday. Got it?"

As soon as she finished, she slipped off her outer layer of clothes. She tossed them aside, and her bedclothes appeared—not the silk nightgown my aunt favors, but a set of long underwear made for spring and autumn. She never sold them because they were oversized, and she's been wearing them so long they're all baggy at the elbows and knees. Clad in these faded pink longjohns, she lay down on the mattress on her tummy and opened her Japanese conversation book.

Sunday morning.

Jin-mo had already woken up and left. I hadn't overslept just because it was Sunday. I was going to do as Mom had asked, but I thought it was too early to feed Jin-mo the chicken. When I looked into his room at 9:20 it was already empty. Maybe some news from his dove had come at dawn or his feeble gang had run into trouble?

There I was, in an empty house, eating a simple bowl of rice in water. Even a small 18-*pyeong* house can feel hollow and lonely when you're by yourself. But it wasn't so bad. I knew that the phone would ring for me within an hour. Of course it could only be one of two men, but I didn't know which one it would be. I had told them both I had to work Saturday night and to call me Sunday morning if they felt like seeing me.

I really didn't have much other choice. I still haven't figured out who I prefer. I'm not so shameless that I'd date two guys at the same time and then make a fuss about it, but this was very important. Just as I had sworn so solemnly to myself that day, I was no longer the An Jin-jin who was living aimlessly. I had already decided to put all my energy into my own life.

After the day I made the vow, I began to ponder everything more and more deeply. I grew accustomed to carefully observing what was going on, no matter what I was doing, even if it was just taking a step backwards. It was the same where men were concerned—I was always watching carefully. I decided to retreat a step until I could figure out who I wanted. Sit on the fence. That's

---

7. *Hiragana* is a form of Japanese script used to write words of native origin.

what my policy would be for the time being. I couldn't choose one of them and set a date for the weekend ahead of time. It was an emergency measure on my part, but I thought it would be okay for me to just wait and see how fate would intervene. If I couldn't make up my mind, then, well, I'd borrow the help of a greater force for a little while.

I ate my rice, washed what few dishes there were and put the telephone down in front of the bathroom. I began shampooing my hair. Still no ring. Well. I changed the rules for the day. I would dry my hair, do a basic make-up job, and get ready to go out quickly, as usual. Finishing all that would take about twenty minutes. If no phone call came in that time, then so be it. Waiting around at home until the phone rang would violate the rules of the game. If there was no call by the end of twenty minutes, then my lot for the day was to see a movie and go to a bookstore by myself.

With just five minutes left out of the designated twenty, the phone finally rang. I already had my keys in hand and was putting on my shoes. I let it ring five times and then picked up the receiver.

"Hello."

A close game, even if I was just playing alone. I was so curious which of the two it would be that my voice almost cracked.

"Hey, Jin-jin. It's me. How've you been?"

The man who had called five minutes before the time limit was up was not Kim Jang-u, but Na Yeong-gyu. If it had been Kim Jang-u, he would have said "An Jin-jin," not "Jin-jin." Unconsciously, I drew a sigh and shifted the receiver from my right hand to my left. I grabbed a rag with my right hand and wiped off the dust that was smeared on the tip of my shoe. And I answered Na Yeong-gyu. Cheerfully.

"Yeong-gyu! I'm fine."

"Can you meet me right now? Please hurry. The weather is terrific."

Sure enough. The weather was perfect, and Na Yeong-gyu was his usual animated self, like a fish leaping out of water.

"Here's the plan. In twenty minutes go to the subway station near your house and wait in front for me to drive up, okay? I'm sorry, but there's nowhere to park. Please get there first. I'm leaving right this second!"

And with the phrase "I'm leaving right this second!" his voice vanished. Questions like "Can you make it in twenty minutes?" or "Exactly where by the subway entrance should I wait?" and detailed explanations didn't suit Na Yeong-gyu. Kim Jang-u would have acted differently.

I hesitated a moment. Fifteen minutes would be enough to make it to the subway, even if I walked slowly. I could have left then and waited, but somehow I felt very uneasy. Idly, I picked the phone up and set it back down again. I examined the polishing job on my shoe tips closely. I took out a compact from my purse and dabbed my forehead and cheeks. Finally, since I really had nothing else to do, I poured myself a full glass of cold water from the refrigerator and drank it. And then, as though it had just been toying with me up until that point, the phone rang. I put my hand on the receiver, took a sharp breath and counted. Two, three, four, five.

"Hello?"

"An Jin-jin! So you're there after all."

Kim Jang-u. Fate had placed five minutes between the two calls. To reconfirm this fate, I had not run out to the subway station.

"Yes, I've been here."

"Well, can you wait? If I get ready to leave now, I can reach you in about an hour. Figure out if there's any particular place you want to go and tell me when I get there."

"I can't."

"How about if we meet in two hours then?" Jang-u, in his ignorance, thought it was simply an issue of time. I sighed to myself.

"It's not that. I've got an appointment and was just on my way out the door. You should have called earlier . . ."

The words in my head tumbled from my mouth without my realizing it. Jang-u's brief dejection was obvious. My reaction the moment I felt that he was hurt surprised me. No, this won't do, I thought to myself. If this was the way it was going to be, you shouldn't have left things up to fate. I shook my head. Probably—no, undoubtedly—if I had made a date with him first and then Yeong-gyu had called, I'd have felt the same. There was absolutely no reason to pay attention to my reaction.

"So . . . well, should we meet this afternoon? I can wait. Just give me a call."

"That'll be hard. Don't wait. Let's just meet next time."

"Okay . . . well, go ahead. Your friend will be waiting. So long, An Jin-jin."

Friend? Jang-u used the word without suspicion. After hanging up I stared at the phone for quite a while. And then, I left home in a determined manner and walked slowly towards the subway station. This game of trying to decide between two men was harder than I thought it would be . . .

I was late. Na Yeong-gyu told me he'd been waiting ten minutes. I didn't make any excuses. But by age twenty-five even a slow-witted girl has a trick or two up her sleeve—as soon as I thought I was within his sight, I broke into a run. That should have taken care of it.

"Why don't we head out of Seoul first and enjoy this gorgeous spring weather? Then we can go to a fancy restaurant and have a delicious lunch. After that we'll take a walk and if we see a nice cafe, we can have tea.

Afterwards, we'll go to Jongno to see a movie. It's okay if we eat a late lunch, right? I bet it is. Most people eat breakfast late on Sunday."

I didn't answer. Okay because I would have had a late breakfast or okay because he had? I couldn't tell which he meant. He was engrossed in his driving and his announcements, with no concern for me. The plans for the day were as meticulously detailed and thorough as the man himself. My opinion wouldn't be required until the restaurant menu was in front of us. But actually, given our track record, I couldn't be too optimistic about that either, because we have almost never gone anywhere that wasn't well-known for some specialty: "This place is famous for its steak." "The ox-tail soup at this restaurant is renowned." "Everybody says the cold noodles here are top-notch."

"The movie starts at 6:40. I bought the tickets yesterday. Dinner will be at nine o'clock, then. Don't worry, though—I know an excellent restaurant in Jongno. Right now we can head to Munsan and then to the Imjin River. On the way back, we'll go through Jangheung, and I figure that we can chat over a cup of tea somewhere around there." Not until he had finished announcing our schedule did he turn to smile at me brightly.

His smile proclaimed complete satisfaction with what he had just announced. It's a very infectious smile. I burst into a grin and smiled back at him in spite of myself. There's something about him that made it impossible for me not to smile, despite my irritation at his one-sided decisions. Round eyes. Maybe it's because of his round eyes. They sparkle with mischief and intelligence. The curve of his double lids gives him an easy-going look. Beneath his eyes is a well-shaped, flawless nose that betrays no sign of life's hardships. The line of his lips is equally delicate. If it weren't for some bluish patches showing that he had shaved, you wouldn't even be able to tell he'd sprouted facial hair.

"There are some snacks and drinks in the back seat. Have a look and help yourself. I was really busy this morning. I had my car washed and went to a public bath to spruce myself up for you. See—we've got a full tank. I filled up because it's hard to find a gas station out in the country. I didn't call you until I had finished getting everything ready. Look at me, Jin-jin. What do you think? Pretty sharp, huh?"

He leaned towards me.

"Yes. Terrific." I gave the answer he wanted even though I thought he was behaving like a little kid.

"You know, I think women's intuition is much more developed than men's. This morning my sister grabbed my arm and said, 'You're in love, aren't you? Who is she? You'd better introduce her to me or else.' Boy, she's psychic."

"Well, what did you tell her?"

"I 'fessed right up. I'm no match for her. My mother probably knows by now too. My sister just can't keep her mouth shut."

I decided to let him know that he needed to watch his words a bit more carefully. This way of hinting that he has decided how he feels and has even been mobilizing the people around him definitely falls into the category of what I consider childish. But whether it's childish is not the issue. Maybe he's made up his mind, but I haven't. I'd be acting hastily if I gave too positive a response.

"Girls always say stuff like that to their older brothers, you know? If I had an older brother I'd say something like that to him every Sunday too . . ."

"What? Uh, yeah . . ."

Na Yeong-gyu, momentarily at a loss for words, unsure what I meant. An Jin-jin, acting nonchalant, turning and looking out the window. Na Yeong-gyu, pretending to be intent on driving, mulling over what I said. An Jin-jin, soon becoming very curious, wondering how he interpreted all this.

He piped up as we passed Gupabal. "That's right. You don't have an older brother. Don't worry. I'll be your big brother, okay?" [8]And he smiled brightly again now that he had delivered this absurd interpretation of my words. I smiled back at him, but inwardly found myself shaking my head. I studied his confident profile as he drove. His response wasn't so far-fetched after all. Wasn't such an answer actually a very fitting defense? Hmm. He wasn't so easy to handle. I'd have to be careful.

A beautiful May Sunday. I steeled myself and got down in earnest to the business of a date. This man with the round eyes rummaged through his tape box at odd intervals, eager to provide us with music, and took it upon himself to comment briefly on each passing scene.

Honestly, why shouldn't I be able to enjoy a drive through the countryside, taking in a feast of green, on a beautiful May weekend? Time spent with a man who has already declared his love to me in various ways to boot. Average people don't make all that many demands about the love they want to receive. If it weren't for Kim Jang-u, it would have been easy enough to come to love Yeong-gyu, at least, inasmuch as he had no absolutely fatal flaw.

Na Yeong-gyu had no truly fatal flaw. That was the problem. That was why I studied the fine features of his profile and smiled at him quietly, as he concentrated on driving along the winding, newly built road. We had a nice lunch at a restaurant built to resemble a traditional log house. He seemed to stumble upon it by accident as we drove merrily along, but actually he had

---

8. The term *oppa*, which literally means a female's older brother, is often used figuratively in Korean, including within romantic relationships.

painstakingly sought it out in some book like *Fine, Fashionable Restaurants on the Outskirts of Seoul.*

"I racked my brains to figure out a route that would have us passing by right about the time you would get hungry. It's really fun making plans like that. I feel like I've taken control over time when things work out the way I want."

Likewise, we happened to successfully "stumble" across a fancy cafe for a cup of tea, when in fact he had done his research and selected it before we even left Seoul. If Yeong-gyu did have a flaw, it was his incredible eagerness to emphasize again and again how cleverly he had planned everything.

"Beautiful, isn't it? The scenery is great, but the reason I chose this cafe is its name, 'That Afternoon.' Some day long from now, we'll be able to reminisce about how we sat and had tea 'that afternoon.' The name is perfect."

He was even planning his memories in advance. The arrogance of his energy irritated me a little. Here he was, working out what he'd remember in the future, and he still had enough juice left over to handle the present without any problem. But I didn't say anything to spoil the mood like "You don't plan memories—they come from what's in your heart" or "Gee, you must get tired racking your brain over such trivial stuff." Why say things you don't need to? It's not just money we should be careful with. Maybe what we really need to spare are thoughtless words.

At any rate, the energy of Na Yeong-gyu, he of the round eyes, was prodigious. He had so much there wouldn't have been any point in his holding even a tiny bit of it back. But around the time we had tea and were making our way back to the city, I started to feel tired. I definitely wasn't carsick from all the driving. I love going on road trips. And it wasn't that the day's full schedule had brought me to the limits of my stamina. All I did as I sat next to him was say a few words or laugh or get out of the car and walk a little bit. No woman my age could claim that was beyond her.

Still, I felt tired. The thought of spending four more hours with him for dinner and a movie made me want to jump right out of the car and go home. What bothered me most was that I didn't have the slightest bit of curiosity about what the time with him would be like.

Things would have been much more interesting if seeing a movie was only a possibility. Or, even if we were going to see the movie, it would have been much more exciting if the rest of the day was a blank slate. But he's not one to let events develop on their own. No, for him, a fixed movie should be seen at a fixed time; a fixed meal should be had at a fixed restaurant. And he thought it all too natural to put the finishing touches to the day by driving me home on a route he'd already planned.

But maybe it wasn't right for me to be so judgmental. Give him a chance, I thought. Cautiously, I tested him.

"Do we absolutely have to see a movie?"

"Of course. I put in two hours yesterday getting these tickets."

Not even a second before his answer. I tried another question.

"But isn't it too early to head there now? The theatre is just over there, and we've got half an hour or so."

"No, I've got it all planned just right. It'll take at least ten minutes to park, five minutes to walk to the theatre, another five to buy drinks and go to the bathroom, and two more to find our seats and sit down. So that's twenty-two minutes. If we take it easy for eight minutes, we can be relaxed when we watch the film. Not too early, not too late, just right."

The man is a walking calculator. When I'm with him, reality, and his ordering of it, stands out as clear as day. It's so clear that dreams and imagination have no room to intrude. But, as most people realize, it's much more comfortable to be a guest at a house that is a little bit messy than one that is spotless.

"Look! The movie starts in six minutes. I was off by two minutes."

The first thing he does when he takes his reserved seat is to calculate the two-minute discrepancy with his plans.

"What do you think? The *shabu shabu*[9] here is great, isn't it? Nine times out of ten when you eat out in Jongno you don't find a good restaurant. But don't worry—I know a half-dozen places as good as this."

I sit at the restaurant table and just nod, and I refrain from asking whether his world would be turned upside-down if he had one lousy meal when eating out.

"I'll take you home now. Call your mom and let her know you'll be home in half an hour," he says in the car.

"It's okay," I answer, as he hands me his cell phone. "I'll be home soon."

"I had a nice time. I hope you did too."

When we are parked on the street near my house, he offers his hand for me to shake. His face, reflected in the streetlights, is all smiles, just like before.

"I did. Drive safely."

I lay my own hand on his. And, in fact, there really were a lot of fun moments.

He turned his car around and left. I walked toward the alleyway that led to my house without regret. For some reason the idea popped into my head that there was a blue phone booth in front of the superette at the alley entrance. I rummaged through my bag and found enough coins to talk on the phone all night. The phone

---

9. A Japanese "hot pot" dish made of thinly sliced beef, tofu, and vegetables.

was there, waiting for somebody to come, press its buttons and seal a pair of lips against the receiver. I knew a seven-digit number I could dial without even looking in my address book.

The phone rang twice at the other end and my coins dropped into the slot. He was home. I had planned to pause for a beat and then say hello, but the sound of a machine cut me off before I got that far.

"This is Kim Jang-u. I am traveling in the far south at the moment. Please leave a message. Beeeep . . ."

But I had no message to leave. Jang-u's kind voice swirled in my ears. Being a photographer who specializes in pictures of wildflowers, he's used to packing a light bag and heading off at any time, but I'd never known him to go on a trip all the way to southern Cholla Province before.

This is how I interpreted his phone message: "This is Kim Jang-u. I wanted to spend Sunday with An Jin-jin, but it didn't work out. I'm going far down south, because I feel all alone. I'll be back when I get over my loneliness."

The way I understood his message made it hard for me to leave the blue pay phone. I had plenty of coins. There was nobody behind me pressing me to hurry. And the gently swinging branches of the flowering lilacs were exquisite, their scent spreading into the night with an irresistible subtlety . . .

矛
盾

4 My Father, at Melancholy Sunsets

Never wander a strange road at sunset.
When darkness settles in indigo tones
From the far side of the sky,
Your heart aches
With a sadness you can't explain . . .

Now it's my father's turn.
It's always been hard to talk about my father. I've always been suspicious of the way people who know him (including, it goes without saying, my mother) interpret him in simplistic terms. My father was not a simple person. He himself must have been unhappy that others were so quick to dismiss him without deeper thought. I would have felt the same. It's humiliating to be considered someone who can be summed up so easily, no matter who you are.

This of course goes especially for someone like my father, whose life was made miserable by pondering all kinds of things, even things it's better not to think about. As far as I know his life was a text that no one has ever read accurately, not even once. The lack of understanding was an insult to my father, as well as his curse.

I think I can say that my father was sensitive to dishonor and singularly unable to put up with insults. There are no errors in this statement. I'm sure of it. And if I can take courage from the thought that what I've said so far is the truth, maybe I can say a little bit more about my father. About a man whom some called a drunk, some called a bum, and others simply considered crazy. About a man whose residence registration certificate now reads "whereabouts unknown."

Yes, my dad was a drunk. If you look at the genetic traits Jin-mo and I inherited, that much is obvious. As Jin-mo often says, he is a natural born drinker who can "knock back four or five bottles of *soju* without having his heart skip a beat." In that case, I'm the rare female who can knock back four or five bottles of *soju* with just a slight quickening of the pulse, but it's thanks to my father's example that the two of us haven't grown up to be full-fledged boozers despite our ample qualifications. The life of a drunk, as he showed us, was unbearably rough and impoverished. We had absolutely no desire to live that way.

According to my mother, Dad's drinking promised disaster almost immediately after their wedding. His penchant for alcohol was a spark waiting to burst into full flame. The first time she saw one of his drunken rampages was on his first birthday after they began their life as newlyweds. Let's see—that would make it only two months. Yes, that's right. They got married on April Fool's Day; his birthday is in June by the solar calendar.

My mother played hostess to two groups of guests on that day. My father's workmates were in the main living room, and his friends in the room opposite. Dad kept going back and forth between them and drank a huge amount. Mom was run ragged trying to attend to guests in two rooms, but he spared no effort in helping out, and so, despite all that he was drinking, he carried bowls of soup and trays of snacks for her. She didn't realize he was so drunk until both sets of guests had returned home; his eyes were a little blurry, and his cheeks were red, but there were no other signs of just how much he'd had.

After all the guests had gone, he went so far as to help her out with the dishes. Actually, she didn't even want his help and could have just told him to relax, but instead, while he was putting away the liquor bottles, she spoke up casually, "Could you bring me the dishes from the living room table? There's a tray over there, but please be careful. Don't just stack the plates up."

She turned around and went back to washing the dishes. Crash. At that moment, there was the sound of something breaking, but because she had the tap running full, she didn't realize how serious the situation was. After a while, though, she became alarmed by odd explosions coming from the living room and rushed in. She couldn't believe what she saw. My father, as if possessed, was hurling the plates at the wall.

The wall was splattered with remnants of the food, and the floor was covered with shards of broken dishes. My mother was so shocked she collapsed in the doorway. At that moment a platter of *japchae*[1] came flying straight at her. She barely avoided it, and, unable even to scream, she fled the house, her apron still on, her feet shoeless.

Of course she went back to her parents. She spent the entire month of June in the same room where she had spent her maiden years. My father came over every day and apologized. My grandmother and grandfather—and, even more to the point, my aunt—kept scolding her. What, no slap on the cheek, let alone any curses? All this, just because she had seen a *japchae* dish flying through the air? And so she steeled herself to forgive him. On the way back

---

1. A dish of cellophane noodles mixed with vegetables and meat, often served on special occasions.

home, Mom just kept repeating to herself over and over again, "Right, it's just because I saw a dish flying through the air. That's all . . ."

When she came home, my father said to her between sobs, "When you told me to load the plates on to the tray and bring them to you, I suddenly felt like I was being wrapped up in chains. Really. I couldn't bear it. The living room seemed like a prison, and when you ran in, I felt like you were a guard locking me up. You can't imagine my despair. It was terrifying . . ."

My mother didn't have the slightest inkling of the entanglements the future had in store for her. Pitying her sobbing, repentant husband, she consoled him. "Oh, honey. Have you ever seen a prison guard wearing an apron?"

Up till that point, my mother still bore a strong resemblance to her sister— that line sounds just like something Auntie would say.

My father's fatal error was failing to emphasize to Mom just how terrified he was of life under "a prison guard wearing an apron." If he had, my mother, who is not overly stupid, could have broken off the marriage easily, all the more so because I had yet to come into being.

My father, however, kept those words hidden until the end. Instead he chose a way of life that saw him gentle and thoughtful when sober, but like a recaptured prison escapee who refuses to give up without a fight when drunk. After that June day he sent dishes flying without hesitation; as time went on, even heavy items (including a television) found themselves launched. When he sobered up, he would calm my mother down and rush off to a department store to buy new plates. To replace the 19-inch television he had smashed, he purchased a TV too massive to hurl again. But even though he couldn't lift it, my father knew a thing or two about smashing cathodes. Several months later, he took a flowerpot from the veranda and that was that.

My father's degeneration from heavy drinker to bum was entirely natural. I was five and Jin-mo was three when he acquired his full qualifications for life as a tramp. He found himself out of work, having half quit and half been fired. His more successful friends and his family, taking pity on his young children and a wife who knew nothing of the world, all mobilized to help him get back on his feet when he first lost his job. As is usual with a good-for-nothing, though, within a few years' time Dad repaid the kindness of his relatives with betrayal and rage. He quit the jobs they found for him and squandered the money he was loaned on gambling and liquor. All too often he came home stinking drunk and demanded small change. If he didn't get it, he would turn everything upside down.

Once my mother realized that help was no longer possible, she set up at the market and began selling socks. My father's career as a bum now moved ahead securely. The way I remember it, he seemed delighted to have a source of money he could extort at leisure, even if it was only petty cash. I can still clearly recall how he jumped for joy when his painstaking searches at last turned up the money Mom had hidden inside pillows or seasoning jars in the cupboard, money she had sweated to earn. Actually, young as I was, I would cheer as gleefully as my father did. I suppose you could say that both of us, father and daughter, were simple and innocent.

My father was not an evil man who would seize loot for himself and then pretend otherwise. He had his own code of honor and always shared a portion of the booty with his young daughter. As he put the money in my hand, he would speak mysteriously.

"An Jin-jin. We're sharing a secret now. You keep half, and I'll keep half. Hold on to your part carefully because long from now we'll need to put what we have together. We'll only be able to recognize each other when our two halves match. If they don't, then we're doomed to live forever in sadness without knowing that we're father and daughter."

"Then should I tear this in half?" I asked, waving a bill.

"No, money is for spending, not for tearing. Spend it any way you want."

"Then what are we supposed to match?"

"See this? Here's something you always carry around with you and never forget. Your hand!"

Dad opened his palm and had me open mine. Then we pressed them against each other. My little eight-year-old hand and his thirty-eight-year-old hand were a poor match.

"They don't fit now and that makes me sad. But some day they're going to match exactly. Will you be a good girl and keep your half of the secret until then?"

I nodded eagerly, captivated by my father's words. Until now I've never told anyone that we've each been carrying half a secret that we've promised to fit together someday. But I tried to give the money back to my mother in one way or another, either by paying for bean sprouts or buying Jin-mo's candy. I might have been young, but I still realized how hard she was working in the market to earn that money.

Strangely enough, I don't think I hated my father in spite of all the terrible things he did. Sometimes my pride was hurt, like when he beat my mother. Or when he upended the dinner table, food and all. Or when a call came from the police station and threw the house into a panic, and my aunt had to rush over and bring us to her house. Even if I bit my lips and scowled at him then, my reproaches never lasted long.

The way I remember it, my father was different from other rowdy drinkers, even when he was beating my mother or turning the dinner table upside down. I realize this sounds strange, but his drunkenness had a certain dignity to it.

That's right. There was an imposing atmosphere about him. Even when he was hurling nasty curses, the way he bit his lips and the way the veins stood out on his brow as he poured forth all his energy made it clear that he felt terribly pained by what he was doing. At odd moments he made not only Jin-mo and me, but even my battered mother feel sorry for him for having to do something that tortured him so much. At any rate, I think that's why she put up with him without resisting. Then again, I've never asked.

My father's slow descent from mere drunkenness into a life of vagrancy coincided with Mom's reaching a decent standard of living as a merchant. Each day she took more room in the market to spread her socks out and increased the number of different types she sold. My father continued making off with several bills at a time and coming home when his money ran out. The more he could steal, the longer he stayed away. When he came back, out of the blue, he would look serious and keep repeating the same thing over and over, even though everyone else was silent.

"People don't all have to live the same way, do they? Right, honey?"

He said the same thing to me too.

"Only fools think that everyone has to live the same way. Got that, An Jin-jin? Do you know what I mean?"

And he would keep asking again and again until we agreed. My mother, who had learned a lot about life from working in the market, gave the frankest answer.

"Of course. It's okay even if it's only you that lives differently."

His expression would brighten at her response.

"That's right, isn't it? You think so too? Thanks. I'm a lucky man. Even if you're the only one who understands me, I don't need to ask for anything else. Really, thanks a lot."

On other days, though, that answer might be the start of trouble.

"You don't really believe that. How can a woman like you acquire such wisdom? You're just trying to hurl me into confusion by talking like that, because you're annoyed and want me to leave home for good. Tell me. Give me one concrete reason why it's okay!"

And the house would soon be in shambles again. I bet nobody else could turn happiness into disaster in the twinkling of an eye like my father. He would beat my mother again, as if in torment, and smash the house up.

I also doubt there's a single man in the world beside my father who uses phrases like "acquire wisdom," "hurl into confusion," and "concrete reason" while he beats his wife.

Eventually my father came to be regarded as having a personality disorder. Around that time, when I was ten or eleven, people around me began to discuss whether he should be committed to a mental hospital. I thought I could accept my father's belief that people don't all have to live in the same way, but I was genuinely curious why in the world anybody would live as he did. I didn't think I could follow such a different path if it meant enduring the pain he suffered.

I couldn't say that in front of him, though. He went from gentle to savage, from warm to cold, from laughter to a deluge of tears in an instant. I didn't hate him, and I never once thought he was crazy like everyone else said, but I kept my mouth shut, because I didn't know which version of my father was real. At age ten I swore to myself that I would ask him that question one day in the future, the far future—on the day when we spread our palms against each other's and matched them exactly.

By then my father wasn't coming home readily even when his money ran out, just once every ten days or two weeks. After a certain point he'd stay away for a month at a time. My mother eventually stopped cooking his portion of rice at mealtime.

Jin-mo and I would spend tense nights until Mom came home from the market, wondering if every sound we heard outside might be our father. Actually, there was no reason for us to be so tense. Dad usually came back home just after sunset, when the dividing line between day and night in the sky had gone all bluish, about the same time I'd return from my own wanderings. I was responsible for calling Jin-mo home, washing him up and getting dinner together, so that this young brother and sister could have a basic meal in front of the TV.

On some days I would come home to find Dad had made it back to our empty house before me. He would show up out of nowhere after a month's absence, without any fanfare, and sit on the front stoop outside the kitchen door, staring out at me blankly. Even though I knew that the man sitting in the bluish-grey darkness was my father, my heart would pound wildly every time I saw him like that, pathetic-looking, but capable of turning into a savage animal within moments. At that young age, I simply stood in front of this frightening but beloved father of mine, unsure what to do.

He always spoke first and liked to address me by my full name. "Hey, An Jin-jin. Long time no see."

He spoke as if he were talking to a friend he hadn't seen in a while, rather than his own child. He seemed to enjoy that tone, and I liked it too. Mom would never have talked that way. Only once he had said, "Hey, An Jin-jin," would I go over and sit quietly beside him. One time he put his arm around my shoulders and explained to me why he came back at sunset. His words were very beautiful.

"Never wander a strange road at sunset. When darkness settles in indigo tones from the far side of the sky, your heart aches with a sadness you can't explain... And it's not just your heart that aches. Out pour the tears. I don't know why. An Jin-jin, have you ever noticed the bitter smell that hovers in the sky at twilight, after the brightness of day has passed and before the darkness of night has come? At that time, when it's neither day nor night, and everything around is tinged with dark blue, there's a bitter smell of home in the air, and I feel an irresistible urge to return. No matter where I am, I have to run and run towards home. But in the end I lose . . ."

So my father would return, but unable to bear it for even three days, he would make off with Mom's money and leave again. If she tried to hold him back, saying it didn't matter and that he could do whatever he wanted if he just lived at home, he would smile faintly and spit out under his breath, "You don't realize what an insult that is to a man like me. You give me no choice but to leave."

My father felt terribly humiliated by what my mother said, and she felt equally humiliated in turn. The cycle repeated. After hiding an appropriate amount of money in a place that would be appropriately difficult for my father to find, she left for the market, lips pursed. Dad would ferret out the money and leave.

It's only to be expected that you develop a tolerance for anything that happens repeatedly. Over time not only Jin-mo and I, but even Mom, who had been so slighted, stopped feeling any inconvenience in our lives without my father. Instead, my mother grew brave and gradually differentiated herself from my aunt. My father, likewise, in his own way became a different person. He came back just once with each season, and then, when Jin-mo and I got to junior high school, he only came once a year. By the time we were in high school, it was down to once every couple of years. The year I turned twenty he stayed with us for a few days, but then he left and hasn't been seen since. Maybe he developed a tolerance for melancholy sunsets that allows him to remain unmoved, even then.

None of us knows what Dad has been doing since he left home. We don't even have any clues whether he's alive or dead, but we do understand one thing: given that he was quite healthy when he went missing and that during over twenty years of life as a vagrant, he must have figured out how to support himself, "whereabouts unknown" simply means his lifestyle has changed.

My father is alive.

I don't know what my mother or Jin-mo think, but I've never once imagined him dead. He just became strong enough to endure the melancholy of sunsets on unfamiliar roads without returning home. But I know the day is near when he will come back again, even if his return isn't permanent. My hand offers the proof. The time has finally come when he and I can spread our palms against each other's and put together our secret.

矛盾

5 Indistinct Shadows of Love

Why all of a sudden
 Did I think
 I'd only be able to sleep
 If I washed his smelly socks
  somewhere . . .

F alling in love. One month is nothing, because time is so short. Yet one month is also long enough for anything, long enough to bring love to full bloom or to destroy it.

I realized this as June passed into July. During that time amazing developments occurred in my relationship with Kim Jang-u . . . and in my relationship with Na Yeong-gyu.

I realize that that remark is going to be met with sarcasm. People won't be able to restrain themselves, "Oh, how trite. You're confessing that you've fallen in love with two men at once? . . ."

No, not at all. I've never been able to stand childish melodramas that are spiced up with troubles or the misplaced way people worship tragic love.

There's no point in saying any of this. I'm talking about love now, but I've got everything completely out of order. Yes, during the last month things have really progressed between Kim Jang-u and me . . . and between Na Yeong-gyu and me, but those are just developments in affection, not love. I don't think I've enrolled in the school of love yet.

I can't even say for sure that a day will come when I'll be able to say "I love you" to anyone with a straight face. I might not have the blindness love requires. Nevertheless one love that is not blind is about to begin right now. But I'm going to have to keep mulling it all over, and I'll have a hard time deciding between the two of them until the last moment. That's the cost of a love that isn't blind.

I realize I'm bringing this up out of the blue, but on Sunday morning there is a matchmaking show on TV with young men and women. I have my own private method of watching, which is really fun. I don't watch the show all the way through—it's much more interesting to watch just the beginning and the end. What you have to do is concentrate on the part when the men and women introduce themselves. After hearing them do the little intros they've practiced and polished a hundred times, I then match the contestants up quickly in my own head and change the channel. I go back to the program just when the screen shows the arrows they've drawn to indicate who they've chosen. And I become tense. I have a great time seeing how I've done with my guesses.

At first most of my predictions turned out wrong. It was strange. I even felt betrayed when I saw couples I didn't think belonged together bathed in the confetti that dropped from the ceiling. Gradually, though, my guesses became more accurate, and now I invariably get at least half right. What I realized is that the contestants worry that the arrows they draw may not be reciprocated, and so they select their second choice rather than their first. And if they aren't hedging their bets like that, then they're choosing partners who seem to be at a similar level of desirability. So a lot of times God's apparent gift to women (or men) comes up empty-handed, and even contestants who aren't especially attractive find a match without problem.

Watching the show like that is fun, but these days it's making me confused. I set the two men in my life down and draw arrows toward them from time to time. First I try drawing an arrow carefully toward Na Yeong-gyu, but I flinch and erase it. Is he just second choice to Kim Jang-u? Next I draw an arrow straight towards Jang-u. Does this mean we're at a similar level of desirability? I can't draw two arrows. I'm caught in the trap I've set for myself.

While I was in the middle of all this, however, Yeong-gyu, without any trouble, drew an arrow pointing straight at me, and that's precisely what's made this last month so meaningful. He's already declared that he's made up his mind; he said he's felt that way about me from the beginning. Kim Jang-u, on the other hand, has simply left the faint trace of an arrow—and hesitantly. That's how he's been from the start.

Indistinct lines.

To explain Kim Jang-u, you have to start with indistinct lines. You'd be wrong, though, if you took this to mean that there's nothing striking about his personality or that his features are indistinct. Not at all. His character is surprisingly strong and he has sharp, fine features. You'd easily pick him out in a crowd. People tend to remember his gentle smile and his eyes as particularly impressive.

A love for the indistinct.

Maybe that would be a more accurate way of putting it. Favoring weakness over strength, seeing the hazy before the conspicuous, preferring subtle scents to the strong . . . a love for all that is vague in this world. Kim Jang-u approaches life through some sort of Zen riddle. That's what I think. And that's why he can't face the world and let an arrow fly directly towards its target. Only when he is unable to cope with the love that fills him—and after a long time at that—does he draw a single, fuzzy line.

When he came back from his ten-day trip to the deep south of the peninsula last May, Jang-u, for the first time, gave me some photos of wildflowers as a gift. The photos themselves paint a clear picture of his love for the vague and indistinct.

"These wildflowers are called 'threadgrass.'[1] Aren't they beautiful? They're thin as thread and white as snow. The flowers bloom in a row and face the sky. Would you believe something so delicate grows among rocks?"

Their petals looked as though a single breath would scatter them like snowflakes. He traipses up and down mountainsides in search of flowers as frail as these.

"And these are called 'milkswallows.' They're very hard to find. I was lucky to get some shots. I like them because they're simple and unsophisticated, just like their name."

The prints showed five blossoms nestled among thick oval leaves.

"These are 'meadowstars.' I had just crossed a stream and was about to move on when I saw them on the mountainside . . ."

He was unable to continue for a moment. Looking up in surprise, I saw that his eyes were moist with traces of tears.

"These flowers were glistening, hidden among the green leaves. An Jin-jin, I was moved to tears because they were so small, so delicate, so peaceful. . . Or maybe it was the idea that they were so beautiful, but hidden away."

Embarrassed, he added, "The picture doesn't capture even half their beauty."

Jang-u loves all mountain and meadow flowers, but it's the white ones that overwhelm him. On this trip he tried to take photos of white flowers only. Playing with the photograph, he told me that he'd taken five rolls of meadowstars alone. I could sense what was in his thoughts.

"Please give me this shot of the meadowstars."

"Are you moved by these flowers too?"

"Yes, although not yet to the point that they make my tears well up."

"Great. Take it."

"Can I have the threadgrass and the milkswallows too?"

"These too?"

---

1. Botanical name: *chinographis japonica maxim* (Korean *silkkotpul*). The wildflowers mentioned here and throughout the book lack common English names. We have either invented them based on literal translation of the Korean if they are compounds, as above, or simply Romanized them. The botanical name of the "milkswallow" is *viola lactiflora nakai* (Korean *huinjotjebikkot*), while the "meadowstar" is *pseudostellaria palibimana (takeda) ohwi* (Korean *keundeulbyeol*).

"I know you brought them for me. This is the first time you've come with your pro photos."

"I did bring them in case you wanted them . . ."

He placed them carefully into an envelope and nudged them towards me. Then, clearly feeling awkward, his eyes darted around. I become more direct when I am with him. He loves things that are vague and sometimes I can't stand them.

I hung the picture of the meadowstars in the center of my wall that very day. The threadgrass and milkswallows went up on each side. Kim Jang-u. A man who wanders mountains for ten days to capture photos of flowers, flowers so delicate they look as though their white petals would scatter at the first gust of wind.

We've been meeting frequently since I hung the photo of the meadowstars up in my room, but come to think of it, our time together is mostly thanks to my acting above and beyond the call of duty.

"It's Saturday. Are you working a late shift today too?"

That's what Jang-u says when he calls me on the phone. Yeong-gyu would just blurt out, "Jin-jin, it's Saturday. Come on out. I'll buy you something yummy for lunch."

"Well, where should we meet? I can't think of anyplace all of a sudden."

If I'm first to suggest meeting, he falls silent, contemplating where we should rendezvous. I hear faint breathing on the other side of the line while he is lost in thought. Yeong-gyu would make a snap decision: "I'll see you in an hour at the New York Bakery."

"What shall we eat? Whatever you want is fine."

Na Yeong-gyu would have already sought out all the fine, fashionable restaurants in the neighborhood; with Kim Jang-u food becomes trivial.

"Well, where should we go now? How about a movie? Let's see . . . is there a movie theater near here?"

After lunch we wander around and eventually decide to see a movie. Then we wander some more. If in the end we do come upon a theater, we're inevitably greeted by the words "sold out."

"Everything worth seeing is already sold out. Oh well. Let's walk around. If we get tired, we can have a cup of coffee."

It would never occur to him to buy tickets from a scalper. But why complain to him? I can't tell him that Yeong-gyu never takes me to the movies without buying tickets the day before, and, anyway, sometimes the movies we miss out on are ones I've already seen with Yeong-gyu.

Actually, I did hint at my annoyance once.

58 | Chapter 5 Indistinct Shadows of Love

Jang-u likes to quote a photographer he admires who specializes in impressive figure portraits. "The right moment for a picture only comes once. If you feel it, don't hesitate. You have to press the shutter decisively. The real value of a picture lies in how well it captures the perfect moment."
Jang-u recited these lines to me on several occasions. I tried to draw an analogy.
"If you're such a good photographer, why doesn't the rest of your life work out like that? Isn't it the same with everything? Capturing the perfect moment—that's got to be what life is all about."
Jang-u begged off. "An Jin-jin, life isn't a photograph. If you don't think a picture is any good, you don't have to develop it. You can just throw it away. But you can't do that with life."
He has a point. A photo is static, but life is a series of moments that flow into each other without stopping. It's not something you can pause to study closely.
So most of our dates take place on noisy, crowded streets. When our legs get tired, we have a cup of coffee and then the date is over. Once we've had the coffee we're at a loss over what to do. May passed and June arrived. Still, we became much closer, astonishingly so.

And today.
We were sitting at a cafe downtown once more. Sunday. Weather that shouted July. He was about to leave again to take photographs of summer wildflowers for a week, so I changed my policy slightly to spend the day with him. If I stuck to my basic principle of going out with the first suitor to apply for a date, getting together with Jang-u would be almost impossible. Yeong-gyu always, without exception, asked for a date ahead of him.
I fussed over Yeong-gyu's phone call that morning more than I had before. I couldn't so callously ruin the days of elaborate preparations he would have devoted to our date. I'm not that mean.
"I'm sorry. Something has suddenly come up. I can't meet you today. But I have time tomorrow. I'll meet you in front of your company when you get off work. How's that? Would that be okay?"
Yeong-gyu took my fussing cheerfully. "No problem. These things happen. But promise you'll stay with me tomorrow night until 11."
"Of course. Even 11:30 is fine."
Hahaha. His joyous laughter was still ringing in my ears as I sat with Jang-u. For this man, who sat blankly before me spinning his empty coffee cup, I, An Jin-jin, ransomed away my whole next evening.
"Let's go somewhere."
"Where?" He looked up at me in surprise.

"I know a great spot. You drove here, right?"
"No, I took the bus. My car is a pain. It's too old and I feel sorry driving it downtown. It's bad for the environment."
Jang-u had a happy-go-lucky smile on his face as I tugged him outside and hailed a taxi.
"Where are we going?" He asked a second time.
"To your house. Then you're going to drag out that old car of yours and we're going to drive to the countryside. The city is too stifling."
"Okay."
He grinned again. That grin. That grin links together every word he says, everything he does, as though he's drawing a light blue line with a watercolor brush . . .
His old, made-in-Korea jeep is a total junk heap. No surprise, given that he bought it used and has been driving it up and down rough mountain roads for the last several years. And although the outside of the car might have been okay, even Jang-u felt flustered about its trash-filled interior.
"If I'd known we'd end up going for a ride, I'd have spent all last night cleaning it. How embarrassing. You don't mind going out in a car like this?"
I climbed into his jeep, with its scratches and dents. I could put up with beating away the dust and trash that collected on my feet and hands as we rumbled along. That was okay. And I could accept that it didn't really feel like a car. But having to deal with it shaking to the point that the muscles in my face got distorted—that was, in fact, not okay. On top of that, he told me the air conditioning had broken down last summer, but he hadn't had it fixed, because he hates air that's cooled artificially. It was so hot and stuffy that I had to let in the humid air from outside. This meant that I also had no choice but to put up with all the street noise. I hadn't expected our drive to be at all like this. To begin with, we couldn't talk.
"WHERE . . . DO . . . YOU . . . WANT . . . TO . . . GO?" Jang-u practically shouted, as he struggled with the steering wheel.
"TOWARDS . . . MUNSAN! LET'S GO TO THE IMJIN RIVER." I cupped my hands to shout the answer back.
"WHERE?"
I wrote "Munsan" and "Imjin River" with my finger in the dust on the windshield.
I wanted to take exactly the same drive with him I had taken with Na Yeong-gyu, partly because the trip itself wasn't half-bad, and partly because without some such plan it would have been hard to stretch out our time together until dinner.
Things were the same even when we were downtown. I would wait a week and then take him to restaurants that Yeong-gyu, brimming with

confidence, had taken me to. Innocently, I introduced Jang-u to the fashionable teahouses that Yeong-gyu had sought out so painstakingly. If it hadn't been for Na Yeong-gyu, Kim Jang-u and I would have had trouble figuring out to how to spend our dates.

Jang-u's beaming profile showed a blissful lack of awareness. He didn't seem to have a problem with either the street noise or the heat that had long since drenched his back with sweat. Once we left the city and began driving along the quiet highway, everything was fine with me too. Since we had to raise our voices to speak—and since the car's rattling made it hard to understand each other even when we raised our voices, we cut conversation and merely drove along, both staring ahead at the road.

But that wasn't bad either. A comfortable silence took the place of the conversation that had vanished. Every so often I'd look towards the driver's seat and Jang-u would open his eyes wide, urging me to speak up if I had something to say. When I shook my head, he would grin that watercolor grin and gaze straight ahead once more. Na Yeong-gyu has a contagious smile that makes the world smile along with him, but Kim Jang-u's subtle grin gives off reverberations that leave me thinking even after he's stopped smiling.

By the time we arrived at the log house restaurant it was very late for lunch. I had been a bit worried—for the restaurant to reveal itself like a hidden treasure we'd have to take the right roads. Fortunately, though, his rattletrap of a jeep followed my finger's instructions to a tee.

"Hey, thanks, this is great. I'm getting to see a whole new world because of you."

He never asked me who I came here with. I most likely would have. Anyone who's even remotely interested in how the world works would naturally arrive at that question, but Jang-u isn't concerned with how the world works. I wasn't sure what did attract his interest. I'm confident that I'd be able to guess what Na Yeong-gyu would be thinking if he were with me now, but it's very difficult to figure out what is going on inside Kim Jang-u's head—he simply grins his watercolor grin and shuts his mouth right up again.

I sat by the window, just like last time. I ordered steak, vegetable soup, bread and a glass of wine, one after the other, just like last time. Kim Jang-u watched me and ordered succinctly even before the waitress asked. "I'll have exactly the same thing as An Jin-jin!"

I burst into laughter, and he blushed, stroking his long hair. He did the same thing when we first met. He hasn't changed at all during the year I've known him.

Until my uncle got me my position in an office, the overwhelming majority of my jobs were in the service industry. Countless cafes, restaurants and beer halls are looking to hire college women; all you have to do is want the job. I met Jang-u last spring while I was working evenings in a Western-style restaurant in Kangnam.

The owner guided a party of three—a man with unkempt hair, wearing a gloomy safari jacket, and two flashily dressed young women—to a table and then came back and pouted. The reason was simple. She always took pride in her restaurant, which was quite high-class, but the man had complained: "It's so dark in here I won't know if the food is going into my mouth or my nose."

"What's an ignoramus who doesn't know a thing about indirect lighting coming here for, anyway? He's better off somewhere with fluorescent bulbs and beef and rice soup."

I went to take their order, and the two women each chose different full-course menus. It took a long time since I had to get the particulars of each item they wanted. Finally I turned to Mr. Safari Jacket. As I was bowing politely, he spoke up without even looking at the menu.

"I'll have exactly the same thing as Section Chief Son!"

"Excuse me?"

At first I had not understood the words "Section Chief Son," but while I was hesitating, he piped up again, "Then, the same thing as Manager Lee!"

I learned later that the two young women with him were managers at a children's book publisher that had bought his photographs. But something embarrassing happened after the meal. I still remember the exact amount of the bill—124,000 won. One of the women acted as if she came to restaurants like this frequently and ordered an expensive wine. If it hadn't been for that, the money he had with him might nearly have covered the meal. He blushed as he handed over eight 10,000 won and five 1000 won notes, placing his national resident identity card on top. "I thought this would be enough. I'll pay you back first thing tomorrow."

The women had already gone out, and the owner was sitting at one of the tables with a friend who had come in the meantime. The big-bodied man waited for my decision. His hands were thrust deep into the pockets of his jacket. I returned his identity card to him without a moment's hesitation.

"My name is An Jin-jin. Just look for me quietly when you pay the money back, okay?"

He studied my face silently and then, without so much as a word of thanks, shuffled out of the restaurant. Right away I found my wallet and put the amount he couldn't pay into the register. The incident took place without anyone being the wiser.

He made sure to return the money the next evening. This time he grinned and thanked me, and even showed up again the following day.

"I thought I'd eat here . . ." he said, grinning again. It didn't bother me that he had come back; his smile was genuine. I carefully pointed out the cheapest meal on the menu, and he ordered what I recommended. Three days later he returned. There was no doubt why he had come. It was all too obvious that he had no interest in what he was eating—he said nothing even though I brought him different food from the last time and he barely looked at his plate. Instead his eyes chased after me as I bustled about the restaurant.

"What was it that interested you in me back then?"
Jang-u knew quite well what I meant by "back then." He contemplated a moment, stroking back the hair that covered his forehead. I might have considered the question childish, but he answered me thoughtfully.

"I just had a sudden hunch when you said, 'My name is An Jin-jin. Look for me quietly.' A hunch that told me I'd be saying your name quietly for a long time to come. It was the first time a woman ever gave me that feeling. My sweet, sweet An Jin-jin."

I flinched. I wanted to become sweeter for a man who called me his sweet, sweet An Jin-jin, and I swore I could not betray such a man. "My sweet, sweet An Jin-jin." That was his mantra with me.

But I'm not sweet. Proof? A glance at my scheming will do. I chose a country road that took us to the cafe "That Afternoon" after we ate at the log house restaurant. Or how about when I paid the bill at the restaurant? I was afraid he might be caught in an embarrassing situation again. His only reaction was an expression that said "oh" as he shuffled out, and I could not hold back a flash of anger.

But how could I be mad for long at a man who shouts for joy when he finds clusters of purple *bibichu*[2] growing in a parking lot flowerbed?

"An Jin-jin, come look! *Bibichu*! And they're already blooming!"
He rushed to his car and came back with his camera bag.

"I might be able to get some good shots. These must be *ilweol bibichu*. Yes, definitely. You can tell because their blossoms are right next to each other. Please wait a few minutes. *Bibichu* droop when they're past full bloom, so they're not as good. Somebody must be taking special care of them. I wonder who? Not a single petal has wilted in the sun. "

Joy was written all over his face as he positioned his lens among the flower clusters. I stood in the shade, watching him work for the first time. I wondered if he gets so overcome with excitement that he talks to himself

---

2. The botanical names for the *bibichu* and *ilweol bibichu* are *hasta capitata* and *hasta capitata nakai*, respectively.

when he is alone in the mountains. The sudden discovery of a small, plain blossom like a meadowstar after a day spent wandering in search of hidden wildflowers can move him to tears. He can weep as he strokes a flower and murmurs to himself in astonishment over its solitary beauty.

Thanks to the *bibichu*, we didn't arrive at "That Afternoon" until the sun was sinking into the hills to the west. The wind was cool, and the twilight sky was glowing—the most beautiful time of day for "That Afternoon," and a piece of luck difficult to come by for those with schedules to keep and who have to be downtown at a fixed time to see a movie at a fixed time and eat dinner at a fixed time.

Although the cafe had an out of the way location, it was filled with young couples. They sat by the window, reveling in their good fortune, their noses pressed up against the glass as they lost themselves in the crimson afterglow of the summer sunset. Sounds drifted in the air—a violin rendition of Edward Elgar's "Salut d'Amour," sweet whispers, soft laughter like splashing drops of water. Maybe they will reminisce about it all sometime long from now— we shared "Love's Greeting" there on "That Afternoon." That afternoon was truly very beautiful.

Braving his rattletrap and the sweltering heat to come here had paid off. The thought put me in an excellent mood. After drinking two nice cold bottles of beer in quick succession I was in a state of near bliss. I sank deep into the plush sofa and closed my eyes. This might have been the first time I had felt so relaxed sitting like this with a man. I had a passing thought—could this be love?

"It's because of the mountains that you feel so relaxed, because you got out of the city." He spoke as if he had read my mind.

"When I get back to Seoul after a few days in the mountains, it takes me a long time to readjust. I want to go back. It bothers me to think about what I've left behind—the bird song, the wind rustling in the grass and skimming across valley streams. I always feel uneasy in cities. That's not where I belong."

He was working on his second bottle of beer and paused a moment to drink. He'd be fully sober and able to sit at the wheel in about an hour, I thought.

"But there are a few reasons why I have to come back. Until lately my brother has been the most important one. I don't want to leave him alone. But these days it's you. Silly, huh? I come back to the city because of you. Whenever I think about you, I want to hurry back."

I understood what he was trying to do. He was trying to draw an arrow in my direction. It wasn't as obvious as the one Na Yeong-gyu sent, stripped as it was of figures of speech, but it was much clearer than the hints he had dropped before. Coincidentally, at that very moment the tape completed a full round, and "Salut d'Amour," which had been playing when we entered, started again. So maybe I'll be able to have my own memories some day far, far in the future. That afternoon I also cautiously shared "Love's Greeting."

At "That Afternoon" we talked a lot for the first time in a long while. He mentioned in passing how much his brother worries for him about his marriage prospects. The two had lost both their parents while young. They had lived together, supporting each other, but recently Jang-u had taken a room on his own. The brothers were parents and family—the whole world—to each other.

I already knew the rough outlines of his past. Jang-u didn't realize that to win a girl you had to disguise that you'd had a hard life and that you were very poor even today. Neither did he realize you could be like me and hide things by trying, as far as possible, not to talk about your family. That way you avoid lying. But he went so far as to say, "The money I earn in the future doesn't belong to me. I should give it back to my brother—because of me he couldn't even go to college. All the money I make is his."

At first his words struck me as very touching, but who knows how long I'll feel that way? Nonetheless, for now they still remain beautiful to me.

"I used to wait up every night for my brother when we shared a place. I didn't go to sleep until I'd washed his dirty socks and hung them out to dry. I felt a sense of peace when I scrubbed his smelly socks, socks that stank even more because he sweated so hard on my account. Even now, I wash his socks sometimes when I visit without letting my sister-in-law know."

Sweet, sweet Kim Jang-u. I had one drink after another at "That Afternoon," but thanks to my father's genes I didn't get drunk. Even so, after paying the bill Jang-u hurried over to take my arm and help me walk. There really was no need. My heart got warm, but my color didn't change one bit. Me, An Jin-jin, get drunk on something as lightweight as beer? I'd consider that humiliating.

We got back into his junk heap and drove off. The only thing on the country road was a row of lonely streetlights; few cars passed. Wind blowing in through the window tousled Jang-u's hair. Every so often he turned to look at me.

"What?"

He grinned. "I want to see if you're drunk."

"Stop the car for a second," I cried.

"Stop? What for?"

He looked at me in surprise as he stepped on the brake and brought the car to a halt at the side of the road.

I had been slumped down in the seat, but sat up straight. I spoke deliberately. "So I can act drunk."

His eyes widened as I drew closer and then he stiffened as I set my lips against them. Then I let my lips settle on his prominent nose, and then on his own lips, which were agape with surprise. His breath smelled faintly of beer. He placed his arms around me tentatively. I was stunned at how wildly they trembled.

I don't remember what route we took to get back home that night. The lamp in front of our gate illuminated my watch. Not even ten o'clock. I felt a brief shock—it was too early for a man and woman who have shared love's greeting to part.

I giggled, leaning against the wall next to the gate. Why did he think this was the only place his old car could set me down? Why all of a sudden did I think I'd only be able to sleep if I washed his smelly socks somewhere? . . .

矛盾

6 The Meaning of Those Ten Minutes, Long, Long Ago

*Coming of age
Means nothing but learning
How to compare your possibilities
with others'.*

The swelter of July passed. As August came on, the heat eased, and in spite of the season, the early mornings and evenings were actually cool. People said it was an abnormally cool summer. Last summer, the heat was absolutely scorching. The weather bureau said it was abnormally hot. I guess that means anything excessive is abnormal.

"*Moo sorosoro aki desu ne. Odenki ga ii desu ne.*" (It's already autumn. The weather is beautiful, isn't it?)[1]

My mother planned to open her shop in September, but the sentences she was practicing so she could do business with the Japanese fit August just as well. But no matter if the weather was behaving strangely or not, my mother kept muttering her Japanese as she washed and ate.

"*Irasshyaimase. Hoshii mono wa minna soroete imasu . . .*" (Welcome. We have everything you're looking for . . .)

One night, when my aunt called, Mom answered the phone with "*irasshyaimase*" instead of "hello," and then laughed heartily.

"I'm learning Japanese. Why? Because it's essential for an international businesswoman. Of course, a privileged woman like you wouldn't know a thing about that. Anyway, get to the point. What's up? Why are you calling me at home?"

I got the sense that my aunt was protesting on the other end of the line.

"When did I say I'm always busy? You're the one who always calls when I'm dealing with customers who want to buy a dozen pairs of socks. Not one pair. A dozen. When somebody wants a dozen pairs, how can I find time to relax and chat about nothing?"

---

1. The Japanese phrase actually translates as "it's almost autumn," but the Korean translation in the text reads "it's already (*beolsseo*) autumn."

I had handed the phone to her, but I had no intention of leaving the room. Although Mom cast a sidelong glance at me, I didn't budge. She knew that Auntie and I have a special bond. My aunt gets information about what goes on at our house from me and vice-versa. If it weren't for the two of us, our families would have been even more estranged. But Mom would not have heard that I had bought a bouquet of roses for Auntie on her wedding anniversary. My aunt is more thoughtful than one might expect.

"We're invited to dinner tomorrow. Ju-ri and Ju-hyeok came home a few days ago, and I said yes. Your aunt has a sixth sense when it comes to knowing when the market is closed. Well, why not? At least your uncle won't be there."

She tried to pretend she was uninterested even as she passed on the invitation. That's her style. She acted as if it took the combination of all three factors to make her go: Ju-ri and Ju-hyeok were home from overseas, the market wasn't open, and Uncle was away on business. If not . . . she's always like that. Communication between the two is impossible unless my rich aunt kowtows to my poor mother. Mom says Auntie has changed, Auntie says Mom has changed. As far as I'm concerned, they've both changed, but I know that they can't escape from each other. That's the fate of a twin.

I don't think it's my aunt whom my mother dislikes, but her husband. And the problem isn't guilt, because she used to accept help from her, even though she doesn't anymore. It's the bitter sediment of the past that has made Mom this way—the bad memories of the days when all too often my aunt had to rush over at a moment's notice to rescue little Jin-mo and me. My uncle's icy stares are still frozen into her memory, his frigid glares when she came to bring us home the following day, once the uproar had died down.

"I'd load you and Jin-mo into Auntie's car. The sky would just be getting lighter in the east when I had finished fending off Dad's kicking and screaming. It took every ounce of strength I had. I'd wait for him to pass out and then rush over to your aunt's like a madwoman. You were in first grade, and if I hadn't collected you at dawn, I wouldn't have been able to send you to school. Do you think I wanted to do things this way? With just one room and the kitchen I had no choice. When Dad started going crazy in such a small house, you'd go hide in the kitchen. Jin-mo would practically have convulsions, he was so afraid. I called your aunt because I was scared all this would kill you two.

"Of course, I've got some sense. I felt so ashamed. Ringing the bell at somebody else's place at the crack of dawn? I wanted to shrivel up and die. But what could I do? I had to ring once, twice, even three times, if nobody answered. Having to be so noisy made me want to die with embarrassment, but Auntie is a deep sleeper. She wouldn't get up right away. Anyway, there was one time, it must've been winter. I waited a bit and then knocked on the gate quietly, 'cause I didn't hear anybody, even though I rang three times. At that very moment, your uncle jerked the gate open. I just stood there hanging my head, like a sinner. But do you know what he said to me? 'Please come in quietly. Ju-ri has her exams today and she needs more sleep. Be careful.' I wanted to crawl into a mousehole.

"And, let's see, when was it? After that I decided I wouldn't go over there until that man went to work, even if it meant you were late for school. But one time I must've been a little early, and he was still at home. You, Jin-mo, Ju-ri, Ju-hyeok and Uncle were having breakfast. And my god. He laid a plate with a nice fat piece of fried hairtail on the table right down in front of himself. Then he took out the bones and gave a piece to Ju-ri, and then a piece to Ju-hyeok. And then another piece to Ju-ri and another one to Ju-hyeok. Jin-mo was staring up at him, wanting some too. I was watching him out of the corner of my eye to see if he'd give him a single bite. But no. Another piece for Ju-ri. And another piece for Ju-hyeok. I was burning up, I was so angry. My poor babies . . . to have to be so humiliated just because you got the wrong parents. I couldn't even think straight."

I don't share my mother's sighs, but the memory of that incident is still with me as well. She grabbed our hands before we finished eating and, clenching them so tightly that they hurt, marched us out of the house without a word of goodbye.

I see my uncle differently than my mother does. Of course, I came to my ideas much later, but I don't think we have any right to criticize him. Ju-ri and Ju-hyeok were his own children, and Jin-mo and I belonged to a drunken brawler. Who would he have loved more? Maybe it was stingy of him not to give us a single bite, but the amount he lent my father was worth one hundred—no, one thousand—no, make that ten thousand times the value of that fish. And even though he didn't get the money back in the end, he never complained. I don't know why Mom forgets all this.

And it's not like I'm being magnanimous just because I've never cared for hairtail like Jin-mo does. People tend to nurse small grudges for a long time, but they're quick to forget bigger acts of generosity. They think they deserve some compensation for the slights they've suffered but aren't concerned about paying back kindnesses. That's how most people tally up the balance sheet of their lives.

On the other hand, Auntie was friendly to her sister's husband, that is, to my father, even though he could hardly have made her sister's life more miserable. Ever since I was young I loved being around Mom and Auntie when they got together and chatted. No matter how often I saw them together,

I never got bored watching two people who looked exactly the same wearing different clothes and with different hairstyles.

The way I remember it, my mother and my aunt got along better when they gathered with the rest of the family at my grandparents' than when they met at each other's house. When they were at my grandparents', they'd hold hands and burst into laughter over nothing at all, like little kids. My grandfather, who had received his daughters on April Fool's Day and married them off on April Fool's Day, loved to have them visit. Just like me, he hated to leave their side. In fact, he was even more devoted than I was. He would look at them from this angle and that, like a sculptor appreciating his own creation, checking for imperfections and fussing over them.

My uncle, born at long last after his twin sisters, was no different. He was still a bachelor and would do whatever his sisters asked. When they got married and left home at the same time, he was so depressed he couldn't eat for three days.

Only Grandmother was busy. The motion of her skirt practically made a breeze as she went back and forth between the kitchen and the outdoor tap to prepare a meal for her daughters. Grandfather would shop for the ingredients himself, and if an item didn't show up on the menu, he'd lay into her. "What's this? What did you do with the chicken legs I bought? Are you hoarding them? I don't see a damn one. Don't you remember how the kids ate ten fried chicken legs last time? How can a mother with any brains forget the chicken?"

"Oh, yes, sure. I'm an idiot mother, and you're a brilliant father. You take your fully grown daughters to the other room and won't let them budge. How am I supposed to do everything all at once? I made *galbi*.[2] I made *jangjorim*.[3] Why should I make fried chicken too? They don't go together."

For the first twenty years after getting married, Grandmother didn't even let her expression change in front of Grandfather, much less talk back, but by that time she grumbled any retort that came to her. And although she may have been grumbling, she was right. She didn't want her daughters to lift a finger when they came home to visit either, and Grandfather always bought much more food than necessary.

But those visits were not always so harmonious. Sometimes—no, inevitably—my father's vices came up and that alone was enough to put a damper on the happy mood. Whenever he was even mentioned, Grandfather, with his hot temper, would cry out, "That son of a bitch." He'd probably have used even more colorful language, but I was a problem, always staring up at him. Despite all the grown-ups' attempts to cajole me into going outside, I

---

2. Beef ribs that are marinated and then grilled.
3. Marinated stewed beef.

Chapter 6 The Meaning of Those Ten Minutes, Long, Long Ago

remained stubbornly at the table. I was a rock of support for my father in keeping him from getting more verbal abuse from his in-laws.

Where my father was concerned, even Grandmother and Uncle just shook their heads. They never visited us at home even once because they hated him so. Compared to my grandfather they were extremely soft and gentle, but at the merest mention of my dad, they would tremble with rage.

At first Mom would get carried away with her own sorrow and criticize Dad hotly as well, wiping her tears away and sniffling as she explained what he had done. The misery on her face acted as a fuse, but my aunt kept the most neutral attitude in the explosion of reproaches that followed.

"He's basically so nice. It's the liquor. When he's sober, he's the sweetest guy in the world. I'm sure he's all torn up about it inside."

"Does a basically nice guy beat his wife hard enough to break her arm? Are all drinkers like that? If he's so torn up about it, then he should pull himself together. If he gave a damn about his wife and kids, he'd give up the booze even if he had to bite his own tongue off."

Grandmother's expression as she spoke was as pained as though she were biting into her own tongue. But it was very strange—even though Mom would be furious to start with, and everyone would chime in with tirades against my father, she would soon change a bit: "He's not that bad. He even washed three blankets for me by himself the next day." What she really couldn't bear was that my aunt was partial to him.

"It's easy enough to take his side, if all you need to do is talk about it. Try living with the likes of him sometime. You wouldn't even last three days. What did you say when Kimpo Auntie was handing around the photos of eligible bachelors? 'It might only be by ten minutes, but you're still my older sister. You go first.' Hmph! That ten-minute difference sealed my fate. If you had been born ten minutes earlier than me, this would be your life instead."

Kimpo Auntie was a distant relative of Grandmother's who played matchmaker for both my mother and my aunt. The man in the first picture she brought became my father, and the man in the photo she brought three days later became my uncle. Grandfather had come up with a blitzkrieg strategy to get them married. The two spent so much time clinging to each other that he figured they'd never meet men and fall in love on their own.

"Don't talk like that. I remember what you said when Kimpo Auntie brought over his picture. 'There's a nice air about him.' And what else? Oh yeah. 'You can see the melancholy of autumn in his eyes' . . ."

If my aunt contradicted my mother in her high soprano voice, then Mom would practically screech at her. "You were the one who came up with that garbage about the melancholy of autumn. You. You're the one who was jumping up and down with excitement about him. You got me all worked up and then fobbed him off on me on the sly. 'Oh, you're older, you choose.'"

Mom was attacking like a rooster in a cockfight. And Auntie, good-natured as she was, would slyly sidestep her and just surrender. "Really? Hmm, well, come to think of it, maybe that is what happened. Right. I liked his looks from the start. But I yielded to you, because you're older. I still don't hate him, though, even now."

Auntie gave in without a fight, but Mom wouldn't let things go until she had let fly a nasty parting shot.

"Yielded to me? Do you know what you yielded to me?" Although several years of marriage had made Mom as fierce as a fighting cock, she managed to choke down the rest—you left me with all this weariness and misery and took all the joy for yourself.

These gatherings at my grandparents' were fun except when my father came up. Mom and Auntie would lie down on a mat on the floor, holding hands, and dawn would creep up on them as they reminisced about childhood. Grandmother would doze on and off, correcting or adding to their reminiscences. Grandfather would be in the next room, constantly going back and forth as he helped his grandchildren to the bathroom. And I would fall asleep as their conversation waxed and waned in the background.

My feelings as I drifted off to sleep had a charm that is hard to explain. Those visits were almost the only chance I had as a little girl to hear my mother talk for a long time without either crying or yelling. I was precocious enough to try desperately to concoct ways for Mom, Jin-mo and me to move to my grandparents', but I always gave up my plans halfway. At that age the idea that I would no longer be able to see my father's melancholy eyes was too much for me to bear.

As my father's behavior continued to get worse, the cozy scenes at my grandparents' became less and less frequent. When someone in the family has troubles that run too deep, other types of happiness are no substitute. Eventually my mother put an end to her visits home.

"No news is good news. Don't worry about me."

Sometimes when my grandparents called, Mom would keep repeating that phrase as if they were the only words she knew. And because "no news was good news" from our house, and all the news from my aunt's was happy, Mom said less and less about her family.

Once my grandfather dropped by our house on the spur of the moment and witnessed one of Dad's rampages. Hot-tempered as Grandfather was, he was on the point of grabbing my father by the neck but wound up falling flat on his back. Grandfather was laid up in bed after that, but before his fall he roared at my father, "Come on, come on, you bastard, have a crack at me."

From then on, even Jin-mo and I, the An brood, were virtually barred from my grandparents'.

My aunt's house was located well off a main street, about a ten-minute walk from the bus stop. For people in her neighborhood, who had cars at their disposal, the farther their houses lay from the noise, exhaust and hubbub of the big thoroughfares, the better.

In summer the days were long enough to be tiresome. The weather was not as sweltering as usual for August, so the evening walk along this quiet street of upper-class homes was not so bad. Green trees poked above high fences and sleek black vehicles crept by from time to time. Not a single mother was screeching at misbehaving children. Someone stood at the end of the street. Auntie's house was just a left turn away from that point.

I immediately recognized Jin-mo. He wasn't the sort of person to be able to enter my aunt's until I was there to ring the doorbell for him. He knew when I left work and must have calculated that I would be arriving at any moment. I had a hard time holding back a tingle of emotion as I walked towards him. It always seems a bit sad to encounter a sibling unexpectedly in some unfamiliar place.

"I'm not going. I can't," Jin-mo blurted out as I approached. It wasn't the usual low voice that he had so readily cribbed from Choe Min-su.

"Why? You made it this far, didn't you?"

But as soon as I asked, I noticed that he looked strange. His face was pale with fright, and the gray-brown suit he had put on for the visit was a mess.

"Do you have any money on you? Give me whatever you've got."

"What's the matter? Something's wrong, I can tell." Alarmed, I grabbed his hands. They were shaking.

"No. I'm just . . . just depressed, that's all. Just give me some cash. I don't feel like going to Auntie's."

He took his hands from mine and made a show of brushing off spots of dirt on his wrinkled trousers. He must have tried to spruce himself up as best as he could on the way, but it was hopeless. I caught the smell of alcohol on his clothes, his hair and his breath.

"What do you want it for?" But even as I asked, I was already taking my wallet out of my handbag. I could sense that the situation was too serious not to give him money.

"I just want to go far away and rest for a few days."

Please let the problem patch itself up after a few days away, I prayed. How likely was it that a novice thug like Jin-mo could get himself in trouble so deep he couldn't get out? I emptied my purse. If I kept this up, how would

I ever manage to save anything? Jin-mo hung his head as he took the cash. It was barely enough to last him a few days.

"Sorry, sis . . ." he added, turning around. "That sweet dove who knew nothing but me betrayed me. Everything's a bloody mess."

When he talked like that, he seemed like Choe Min-su or Al Pacino without really even trying. Truth, it seemed, was speaking after all. As soon as Jin-mo said that his dove had betrayed him I felt relieved. Nothing surprising about that. The only thing that ever happens to Jin-mo is that he betrays some girl or some girl betrays him. What more could happen?

Punishing those who betray your love is simple: forget them. Thoroughly, completely, so that the traitor doesn't even show up in your dreams. I could do that. Maybe Jin-mo could do it even better. His dream of becoming a gang boss may have lost some of its meaning because of the dove's betrayal, but surely another girl would come along and bring that dream back to life.

The time we spent at my aunt's that day was, as Jin-mo would put it, "a bloody mess." Things had already gotten off to an ominous start for me because of Jin-mo, but even worse, Mom couldn't let a single thing go without making a snide comment. She was always like that at Auntie's house, but that day she was over the top.

I understood why Mom was acting the way she was. With her children home, Auntie looked especially beautiful and was overflowing with energy. She was usually happy as a lark anyway, but having Mom and me there too brought her to the height of bliss. In her delight she had decorated every nook and cranny of that big house of hers with flowers. Mom's carping began with those innocent flowers.

"What in God's name did you stick flowers around everywhere for? It looks trashy. Your yard is full of them in the first place. Don't you have anything better to do?"

My aunt likes to pay attention to ambience, but even the gently murmuring music she put on irritated Mom.

"What's with this annoying music and all these new gadgets? You must have blown several million on them. It's beyond me why you buy such expensive stuff when all you listen to is pop songs. You really do have money to burn."

It was true that my aunt liked pop music. That's why she got so caught up in studying piano along with Ju-ri back when Ju-ri started piano lessons long ago. Later, Ju-ri used the skill she acquired to play Mozart, while my aunt went for "Yesterday" or "You Are My Life." Even now, when we asked her, she could treat us to old Korean standards like "Passionate Love" or "I Don't Know What to Do."

Ju-ri spoke up for her mother, who had just been criticized for her musical taste. "Mom, why don't you turn off the stereo and play 'The Thorn Tree' for us? That was really nice." From what Ju-ri said, I guessed that these days my aunt must have been practicing the tune by the popular duo "The Poet and the Village Chief." The songs Auntie prefers are ones that even appeal to someone like me, from a different generation.

My mother did everything she could to pick a fight, but Auntie remained unperturbed, because she was happy. The problem was me. I hated to see Mom act like that in front of Ju-ri and Ju-hyeok. I also felt out of sorts because I couldn't get out of my head the way Jin-mo's hands trembled as I gave him the money. Caught as I was between Mom and Auntie, neither the flowers nor the stereo bothered me.

What did bother me, though, from the very moment I walked in, was Mom's perm. It still reeked of fresh lotion. I could barely bring myself to look at her and her hick hairstyle with its curls frozen in place. Better if she had just come looking the way she did in the morning, her hair disheveled and having lost some of its wave. I would have felt less miserable.

In contrast, Auntie looked terrific. She always paid careful attention to her hair but styled it naturally. Her round shoulders appeared from beneath a charming sleeveless green dress. She had the air conditioning set to just the right temperature, the decor in her living room matched perfectly, and her mustard-coloured leather sofa created an atmosphere of elegance. Only one item was dreadfully out of place: my crabby mother, sitting there with her hair curled into a frizzy perm.

So it wasn't my fault that I made her a sudden laughing stock by bringing up the name of her favorite hair salon. I just wanted her to stop going there. Being at my aunt's made the wish so strong that I simply blurted things out before I even knew what I was doing.

"Mom, don't tell me you went to 'Le Palais de Perm' again today![4] I begged you not to get your hair done there. What did you go again for?"

"What? Your beauty parlor is called 'Le Palais de Perm'?!"

Auntie collapsed to the floor then and there in hysterics. She's never been able to control her laughter. It was one of her weak points. Ju-ri burst into guffaws, clapping her hands noisily. Ju-hyeok also kept glancing at Mom's hair and chortling. The scene was so uproarious that even their housekeeper came running out of the kitchen to join in the amusement.

Mom immediately turned beet red. I had slipped. At our house we no longer even noticed anything funny about the name of the beauty parlor— Mom had been going there so long, it was just a name to us.

---

4. "Le Palais de Perm" is our attempt to capture the humor in the Korean name *"ppokkeulle,"* which gives a mock French sound to the question, "Would you like to friz your hair?"

I felt terrible, but Mom recovered in a flash. Auntie, who doesn't have a malicious bone in her body, kept teasing her, "Did you get your hair done at 'Le Palais de Perm'?" Mom just glared. My mother has never let herself come second to my aunt. When Ju-ri and Ju-hyeok went upstairs, she finally latched on to a new subject to pick a fight over.

"She's studying piano and she says she can't come home during vacations because she has to write papers?"

Ju-ri had said she couldn't come home because of essays, but Auntie had twisted her arm. For Mom to be critical about that disappointed not only Auntie but me as well. The question showed all too clearly how little interest my mother had in Ju-ri. At least my aunt knows exactly what goes on with Jinmo and me.

"You still need to ask? How many times have I told you that Ju-ri stopped studying piano at college and took up Fine Arts."

My mother's questions kept coming without her even realizing the gaffes she was making.

"Is Ju-hyeok at college now or in grad school?" Early this year we heard that Ju-hyeok had graduated with high honors from an Ivy League college. He was now on his way to graduate school, and so both of my cousins were making a mad dash upwards toward the exalted status of a doctorate. I knew very well, though, that what my aunt wanted for Ju-ri and Ju-hyeok was not a Ph.D.; she just wanted her kids to finish their studies and come home to her. But that was hardly possible. For my uncle, that was the desire of an idiot.

"After a bachelor's degree, there's a master's, and then the doctorate. Why give that up? We've already decided they'll get that far, and they've gone to study overseas. I really can't fathom why you have to tell them to stop."

Besides, he went on, they were both excellent students. That's Uncle. Here's an analogy. For almost thirty years of marriage he's been a train that has arrived and departed on time like clockwork. Now, you might expect a train that clatters along winding rivers and hillsides to be cancelled after heavy snow or to be delayed while waiting for another train to come from the opposite direction. Right? My uncle conceived of a train's task differently, though, hard as it may be for most people to understand.

For my uncle, a train should not be distracted for a moment, even if it travels along a winding river, and it shouldn't arrive late at the next station, even if it means colliding with a train coming the other way. But I suspected my aunt's train was not the same as my uncle's. If not, why would she have said to me, "Your boring uncle"? . . .

One thing I can say for sure is that my cousins are different from Jin-mo and me. My aunt was blessed with good fortune, from her husband to her children. In contrast, as I grew up, I heard my mother say hundreds of times that she'd been unlucky not only in her husband but in her kids. Because of Auntie, those words had become inscribed in my heart as gospel truth. Mom had been bested by her sister in both. If, as my mother claimed, the issues of husband and kids were linked, not separate, there was nothing surprising about that.

I had a special relationship with Auntie but didn't feel particularly close to my cousins. Except for a brief period when we were young, we really hadn't had the time for that. And even when we were young, it was difficult to get close to them, raised as they were under my uncle's ironclad protection. Ju-ri and I were the same age. So were Jin-mo and Ju-hyeok. But the only thing similar about us was our ages; otherwise we were completely different. Actually, let me take that back. We had one thing in common—we had mothers who looked and sounded exactly the same.

By the time we had become mature enough to be capable of really getting to know each other, both of them went overseas to study. Even if they hadn't, though, I doubt we'd have managed to create any pleasant shared memories. Coming of age means nothing but learning how to compare your opportunities with others'. Like Mom, I haven't been able to avoid feeling petty about the unlimited opportunities my cousins have. But where I differ from her is that I've been able to go about my life keeping my jealousy under wraps. If it had slipped out here and there, my life probably would have been a complete and utter failure.

My mother's most strident rebellions against the fate dealt out to her and her sister were focused on us, her children. By an unlucky coincidence, the day I ran away from home for the first time also happened to be the day she heard that Ju-ri had won a nationwide piano contest. I learned later from Jin-mo that Mom spent all night slamming her fist against the wall and sobbing, "My poor kids! My poor kids! Only my kids . . ."

At this point, however, she is accepting her fate. And although she seems to have managed to rise above everything else, we are still her greatest weakness. It can't be helped.

That day at my aunt's Mom openly exposed her weak point. She had been struggling to control her criticisms of her niece and nephew, but the trendy clothing Ju-ri and Ju-hyeok had on when they came downstairs for dinner wore out her patience.

Ju-ri had dyed her hair a light brown that verged on blonde. She was wearing a black dress, cut low over her breasts and on her back. Not only that, three earrings studded each of her pale little ears like beetles—six in all.

Mom checked my ears first; I don't wear earrings in the summer, which further fanned her desire to attack. Before long she broke the silence gently.

"With all your studying, how did you find the time to get three holes drilled into each ear?"

"Oh, piercings just take a second apiece."

Unaware what my mother was driving at, Ju-ri answered with an amiable smile.

"You don't go out in that, do you? Is that any kind of dress for a Ph.D. student?"

"Is there something wrong with it? I changed into a nice dress especially because you were coming, Auntie. Don't you like it?"

Ju-ri was still trying to be pleasant but by this point she had picked up on my mother's surliness. She lowered her head and tried to avoid eye contact with her. If Mom had stopped there it would have been enough, but she turned her attack to Ju-hyeok. His awkwardness with chopsticks provided her with the opening she was looking for. When the housekeeper set a knife and fork on his plate, her eyes blazed sharply.

"Don't tell me you've forgotten how to use chopsticks already. Cutting greens with a knife? I've never seen such a thing in my whole life. How are you going to survive when you come back to Korea? That's a worry, a real worry."

Auntie was staring at her son, a rigid expression on her face. Ju-hyeok looked up at her once.

"Don't worry. It's not as though I absolutely have to live here. My friends, my teachers, my memories are all over there. There's no reason to come back."

Auntie dropped the spoon she was holding. Ju-ri was trying to keep her brother from saying more, but he was already continuing.

"And Ju-ri really has no reason to come back. She already has a contract for an important project with a cultural center over there, and she has a guaranteed position at her university as soon as she files her dissertation. It's a huge success no matter which one she chooses."

"He's talking like an idiot. What does he mean no reason to come back? Mom and Dad are here. What could be as important? Right, Mom?"

Ju-ri stroked her mother's cheek and smiled brightly.

"I'm sorry. I don't know what I was saying." Ju-hyeok meekly admitted his mistake.

I quietly picked up the spoon my aunt had dropped. She relaxed her rigid expression and left the table briefly to get a new spoon. While she was gone, Ju-ri gave her brother a dig in the ribs. Ju-hyeok shrugged and went back to cutting the vegetables on his plate with aplomb. Mom didn't bother to pick a fight with him about chopsticks again.

My aunt patted Ju-hyeok's round head lovingly when she returned to the table as if to say, "I'm okay now." Ju-hyeok smiled back at her. With that, my aunt, in her green dress, perked up like a wilted plant made verdant and healthy once more. She was still beautiful.

Nevertheless, at that moment I was able to catch in Ju-hyeok's smiling expression the same formal smile that Uncle had given me at the French restaurant back in April. My uncle's face, the face of a man who'd as soon die as allow cancellation or delay, the face of a man who had taken the excitement out of life, had been transferred intact to Ju-hyeok. Right. Ju-ri and Ju-hyeok were my aunt's children, but they also belonged to my stern uncle. Likewise, Jin-mo and I are my mother's children. But in many respects our father has defined us.

矛盾

7 Wallowing in Misery

*Kneeling in surrender to great misfortunes
   Is far easier
   Than struggling against small ones.*

August dragged on.

From the beginning of the month Mom was busy with her plans to open a new store. September was clearly on its way, and it was no longer very hard for me to imagine her giggling in front of Japanese customers, "*Moo sorosoro aki desu ne.*" Fall is already here, isn't it? Once summer arrived, she had stopped taking new items and sold only the goods she had in stock.

I was making plans to go with Kim Jang-u on his autumn trip once the month was over, so I hadn't asked for holiday time off. I wouldn't have gone anywhere even if I'd received a vacation—I hate summer. It's very trying to remain on friendly terms with the world in oppressive weather, when it's too hot even to breathe deeply. Just waiting for summer to hurry up and finish was more than I could handle.

"In the summer, mountains are a feast of loud, red lilies. But autumn is a banquet of wild chrysanthemums. They come in pure, simple clusters and they're the most beautiful flowers of the season."

Autumn and the feast of wildflowers I'd been invited to enjoy with Jang-u was not far off, but August was not easy to get through. Jin-mo never came home. The month dragged on, as if to let us know that considerable time would have to pass before he could return.

I should have been more cautious when I met Jin-mo in the alley on the way to my aunt's. I had definitely made a mistake in concluding that if he was in trouble it was only because he'd betrayed some girl or vice-versa. And it was clearly my fault for not realizing that, even if it was a problem with a girl, some mishap may have been involved. I should've asked Jin-mo for a few more details at the time. If I had, I'd probably have avoided the scene in that tense and brutal police investigation room, when I had to ask the plainclothes detective again and again what had happened to him.

"It's attempted murder. How many times do I have to tell you? A group of them went in to kill him, and what's worse, your brother was the ringleader. Stop bugging me with the questions, okay? Look, you're his sister. Just cough up all you know about where he took off to. Chasing the rest of those guys down wore me out."

He lifted his hands from the keyboard he'd been typing on and stretched as if to emphasize how fed up he was. The detective next to him cut in.

"What are you talking about? All it took was a little time to play hide and seek. Didn't you just crack the case without even working up a sweat, Detective Cho? The rest of his partners were so sweet that all they needed was one word from you, and they spilled everything. Cute little bastards."

The two detectives had suddenly shown up at our house in the early evening, before Mom had come back from the market. Searching our 18-*pyeong* home was a snap, but I had to go down with them to the station. I'd been to the police box in our own neighborhood because of Jin-mo often enough, but this was my first trip to a station where officers in uniform stood guard with guns. I immediately found myself regretting that I hadn't taken Jin-mo more seriously.

To be honest, when the prosecutor told me the charges against Jin-mo my first reaction was amazement. "Wow," I thought. "It's really big this time. Pretty impressive, Jin-mo." Don't get me wrong, though. I didn't think that just because I had a devil whispering in my ear. Even in the midst of it all, it never escaped me that the accusation was attempted murder, not murder. No one had died. Jin-mo hated someone enough to kill him and he actually tried. But when he was on the verge of actually doing it, his hatred vanished, and the incident had a happy ending. All the victim needed was five months or so in the hospital, and then he'd be able to return to normal life, as though he'd never been the target of an attempted murder in the first place.

I wasn't there to be Jin-mo's guardian the time he was hauled off because he wound up brawling instead of paying for the pork and few bottles of *soju* he'd had at a small bar in our neighborhood. And I wasn't there to rescue him the time all the cops at the local police box repeatedly dug their knuckles into his head. He'd been charged with harassing a woman who had passed by. These are just a few of his minor offenses before he turned twenty. If Jin-mo at age twenty-three, and having already done his time in the army at that, had wanted me to be his guardian when these trivial charges came up, I'd have really been furious. Jin-mo was not the Jin-mo of old.

That's how I worked things out for myself. To my mother, though, what had happened was part of a recurring nightmare. I tried to break the news to her delicately, but as expected, she turned as pale as a ghost.

"It's starting all over again! All over! After your father disappeared, and Jin-mo went to the army, things quieted down and I finally started to relax a little. But now it's happening all over again. This is terrible. Terrible! And murder, of all things. Oh god. I'm so ashamed I could die. The mother of a murderer? I won't be able to show my face anywhere. "

Mom and I were exact opposites. She heard only the word "murder" and ignored "attempted," while I just paid attention to the word "attempted" and ignored "murder." But I couldn't persuade her to do otherwise, no matter how much I tried. She obviously took the word "attempted" as meaningless padding. If it hadn't been there, though, she'd have keeled right over.

Instead of collapsing, what Mom had to do was inflate the misfortune that had befallen her. She already knew from experience that kneeling in surrender to great misfortunes is far easier than struggling against small ones. That's how she's managed to overcome the repeated calamities she has faced in her life.

Mom's penchant for exaggerating misfortunes is a difference between us. It's another reason why I get fed up with her. But I can't blame her. Nobody has a right to criticize someone whose life is constant misery at best. If she goes so far as to wallow in it in order to emphasize it all, it's perfectly understandable . . . I can still get sick and tired of it, though.

The problem now was to figure out, together with the detectives, where Jin-mo was. Ten days had already past, much too long for him to be able to support himself with the money I'd given him. And even if he had money, I didn't want him to be bottled up in some unfamiliar room in an unfamiliar place. That wasn't going to solve the problem. The thought of Jin-mo being in the dark about what was going on and shuddering as he imagined the worst case scenario made the situation even more urgent to me than to the detectives. I couldn't just desert him. Who would make sure nothing happened to him when twilight glowed purple and smoke rose all around from dinner fires? We're our father's children. That hour is our Achilles' heel.

It was clear enough what had happened. Jin-mo's dove had met a guy who knew a thing or two about using his fists, and that's where the trouble started. He must have shown her a much classier side of organized crime than Jin-mo. She didn't do anything wrong. Even I could see that Jin-mo's imitation of gang life was shoddy.

According to the detectives, the victim had been attacked in the men's toilet at a beer hall. He was drunk and could barely walk. At least three men, four including Jin-mo, had jumped him from behind with sticks. Jin-mo must have called out all the reinforcements he had at his disposal.

And according to what the detectives also so kindly related, they had managed to round up the other culprits in Incheon after ten days, and all of them had denounced Jin-mo as the ringleader. They were just following their boss's orders, they said, which, in the event, amounted only to a brief command. "Get rid of the bastard."

I can tell what happened even without having been there. Jin-mo would have flicked the cigarette nestled between his lips into the air and recited his line in that low, gloomy voice. "Get rid of him!" He must have practiced the words over and over again. Maybe he was excited enough to forget for a little while that his girl had betrayed him. I hoped so. After all, everything had seemed like a joke to him. How embarrassing it would be to find that what had started as a joke didn't end as a joke. How strange it would be to come face to face with truth. I intended to offer support for Jin-mo's joke until the bitter end so that he doesn't wind up ashamed about this life.

"He didn't die. We can fix things. Just come back."

That was the first message I left on Jin-mo's beeper. Of course there was no response. A day later I switched back to the way I usually talk and recorded another message.

"Act like a real boss. Your cronies fessed up to everything. Come back and teach them a lesson."

Still no response. The detectives came to our house in the morning and again in the evening to ask me for developments. They stank of sweat from wading through the stuffy August air. Every night Mom clutched at the wall, lamenting her lot as the mother of a murderer. Eventually she would collapse and fall asleep on the bare floor. A week passed. I left a third message.

"Hurry up and come back already. What are you waiting for? Go to the police and give yourself up. Stop giving your lackeys such a hard time and act like a real boss."

The day after I left the third message I got a phone call from Jin-mo at work. I had expected as much. I was overjoyed as I picked up the phone.

"Jot this number down. You can call and turn yourself in."

"Sis . . ."

Jin-mo was crying. I stubbornly persisted in reading out the number.

"How's Mom? . . ."

Mom was an issue Jin-mo couldn't avoid. Just as our father was an issue Mom couldn't avoid, we had to face up to her. I felt a sense of connection to Jin-mo for the first time. I was touched, not so much because of Jin-mo and his situation, as because of this bond, the feeling that we were comrades-in-arms.

And so, Jin-mo returned on August 23rd, although he didn't come back home, of course.

At this point Mom went into action. The past few years had been the quietest of her adult life, and she had managed to stow away a fair chunk of money in her bank account. This became her weapon. First she set about getting the charges against Jin-mo toned down and met with the man who had been beaten up to talk things over.

My father and Jin-mo after him had already trained Mom for what was necessary. She got advice from people in the market who had lots of experience in these sorts of matters and looked after Jin-mo perfectly. With Mom splitting her spare time between wailing and taking care of Jin-mo, there was nothing I needed to do.

She had been getting ready to open up her food store in early September, but her plans were put on hold indefinitely. And even though she wasn't shouting out welcoming calls of *"irasshyaimase"* to Japanese customers as planned, she was caught up in a whirl of activity. Sometimes I'd perk up my ears, half-expecting her to start humming at any moment.

She threw herself into solving the problem so completely that I wondered how she had put up with the peace and quiet of the last few years. Her exaggerated way of grabbing at walls and wailing at the top of her lungs was actually quite useful to her. After blowing up what had happened into as much of a disaster as she could, she escaped from it gracefully. The woman I got to see in August was a master of hyperbole. She truly amazed me.

Yeong-gyu was the man who consoled me during that tedious month. He sensed that something had happened and did everything in his power to cheer me up.

Jang-u was volunteering his services for the summer at his brother's travel agency—not because business was booming, but the exact opposite. His brother couldn't afford to pay an employee at the moment. With his brother's business in a crisis, Jang-u was actually spending a more depressing summer than I was. He didn't hesitate to tell me how down Jang-ho's situation made him, but I never let on in the slightest about what was happening with Jin-mo. Nothing is as stupid as believing that "honesty is the best policy." Sometimes honesty is a boomerang that comes hurtling back at you as a murder weapon.

Oddly, I felt freer to be honest with Na Yeong-gyu than Kim Jang-u. I felt like my own pride was being hurt if I wasn't honest with Yeong-gyu. He knew that my mother sold socks in the market and that my brother was a wannabe gangster who had finally landed himself in a huge mess and been arrested. Nobody knows better than I do how to live without letting on about the truth, but I didn't do that with Yeong-gyu. I don't know why. Maybe I wanted to test him. I'm sly enough to take those risks. I became a gambler who lets everything ride on the last round, winner take all—but even if I lost, I was going to play again the next day.

So Yeong-gyu and I remained in frequent contact throughout that exhausting August. He would wait for me to get off work and take me somewhere new and special. He treats love as though it's a subject he's studying and in this area he has a uniqueness Jang-u can't touch. I began to take pleasure in Yeong-gyu's particular qualities.

"I can pull strings if he's handed over to the prosecution. Don't worry too much—my cousin works over there. Hot-blooded young guys act up sometimes."

As he spoke one day, he clasped my hand. We were in Yangpyeong, in a cafe with a roof made entirely of glass. It was wonderful to look up and watch the heavy raindrops drum against it. Yeong-gyu assumed I was down because of Jin-mo and didn't let the opportunity slip. I pretended to be distressed and let him hold my hand. His hands had a tender warmth and dryness, but I didn't feel the slightest emotion. We sat side by side instead of opposite each other, just like the other couples scattered about the dark cafe.

He became a little more daring, slipping his arm around my waist. The position we were sitting in became awkward, and I didn't have much choice but to cradle my head against his shoulder. He smelt faintly of sweat, faintly of soap. He held my other hand and began to stroke my hair. Wow, I thought, this position is really uncomfortable. It dawned on me that if you really want to sit comfortably with a man you need to turn at a thirty-degree angle towards him, but I didn't. If I had, it would have flustered him, and after all, I, An Jin-jin, show more concern for others than anyone does. I could scarcely do such a thing.

"Let's get married soon. I want to marry you."

At last the word "marriage" popped from his lips. His proposal came three months after he first said, "I really like you, Jin-jin" and two months after he said, "I love you, Jin-jin." He was following the stereotyped order to a tee.

I wasn't surprised—I'd been expecting as much. If I said differently I'd be lying. But I was still a bit taken aback, because I had a responsibility to answer. I hadn't told him not to love me, to stop loving me, when he declared his love. Yeong-gyu was not someone to let my hesitation bother him in the least, however. Even though you can never know if things will go the way you want, he believed I would love him, because he had said he loved me, and he believed that I would marry him, because he said he wanted to marry me.

"I'm ready. Ever since high school I've had it in my head to get married when I was twenty-nine. I thought, I'll usher in a wife in the last year of my twenties. Then, when I turn thirty, I'll truly be an adult. And guess what? I turn twenty-nine today—it's my birthday. If I get married within a year, everything will have gone just the way I planned. Are you following me? Do you see why I proposed to you today?"

He beamed a blissful smile in the belief that his splendid life was unfolding exactly according to plan. I closed my eyes as I leaned my head against his shoulder, still feeling uncomfortable in that position. At that moment, eyes closed, I had a vision of a white slip of paper with neat lettering on it.

"August 27. Roughly ten p.m. Site: cafe with glass roof to create dreamy atmosphere. First hold girl's hand. If no particular resistance, wait roughly ten minutes and propose . . ."

I imagined a memo jotted down for August 26, a reminder of elaborate plans for his life drawn up ages ago. The proposal hadn't surprised me, but a shudder ran down my spine as I envisioned this life plan of his. But even before my shudder had died away, Yeong-gyu suddenly moved lower and covered my neglected lips with his. Yes, the lights were low. And yes, all the other young lovers were wrapped up in each other and paying no attention to anybody else, but still, that kiss was sudden. Sudden and deep. And then I saw it again, that scrap of paper. Its next line read, "After successful proposal, decisive, sudden kiss. Await opportunity. Kiss must be natural, not hurried."

The reason I was so relaxed about letting him kiss me that day is because I was worried I'd embarrass him if I didn't. I didn't want to make this sweet guy feel awkward about something so small, and it was hardly a big deal to put up with the kiss for a second.

No, the kiss was fine. But the life plan that popped up and fluttered in front of me from that day on—now, *that* was a problem. It became installed in my brain as an automatically appearing screen. Every time he said or did anything, a device whirred into motion and projected an enlarged image of his instructions for the day in my head.

All this made it very hard to meet Yeong-gyu. I felt suspicious of him constantly, even if we were just having a bowl of cold noodles. Maybe it was already noted in his life plan that today at this very moment that is what he was supposed to eat. Just how far did his planning extend? Was it possible that even our first meeting was no accident?

When I started at the job I have now, the one I got thanks to my uncle, what gave me the most trouble at first was the computer. After I became a college student, while my other friends were scurrying to institutes and throwing themselves into computer or English conversation classes, all I was concerned with was coming up with tuition for the next semester. Even though

I haven't managed a diploma, as it turns out, registration fees were still my top priority.

I absolutely refused to study on the money Mom earned selling socks, T-shirts and underwear. I made my mind up about that firmly back in high school when I was preparing for college entrance exams. I had vowed to be financially independent, quite apart from whatever Mom may have thought. Back then, I was nervous about whether I'd be able to stick to my vow and didn't have the chance to take computer lessons. It wasn't so much that I didn't have the money as that I couldn't spare the time I needed to earn more.

My heart sank on my first day at work when I saw a huge computer occupying half my desk. The section chief said I'd have things under control in no time. All I needed was to get the hang of a few basic points. But that still left me with compiling all sorts of far from basic documents, typing them up and saving them. Those complicated tasks were all mine.

The company where I was working specialized in importing high quality tiles, floor materials and building stones and distributing them nationwide. All the items were unique in color or design and so different invoices were needed for each. I had to keep track of such things as their arrival at the warehouse, the present state of orders, branch sales, quarterly confirmation of receipts, and the current stock inventory. My predecessor had already left and I had no one to turn to for help. My uncle, being an architect who mainly designed office buildings, was an important customer of theirs, and so they didn't treat me badly. Still, I desperately wanted to avoid being labelled an inefficient new worker, if only for Uncle's sake.

So I had no other choice. My very first day at work, I went out at lunch and registered for early morning classes at a computer institute just opposite the company office, and that's where I met Yeong-gyu. He was taking a more advanced class that met at the same time. I found an empty classroom so I could practice what I'd learned until I had to leave for work. He spoke to me first.

"My name is Na Yeong-gyu. There's a cafe that makes terrific sandwiches just a minute's walk from here. Would you like to join me?"

I was hungry, so I followed him. The sandwiches were delicious—the cafe offered an excellent service for the students attending early bird sessions at the nearby institutes.

Every morning we fortified ourselves with breakfast and went off to our respective companies. Sharing a meal with a man with kind, round eyes was a nice, relaxing way to start the day. I didn't find him unpleasant and, not long after we met, he began saying cheerfully that he was growing fonder and fonder of me. That's how, along with Kim Jang-u, he became the second man who might propose to me—although granted he's already gone and done it.

But what if even that happened according to some grand design of his, planned far in advance? What if there was a memo that read: "Feed sandwiches to girl. Continue to eat together daily for roughly one month. Say, 'I'm growing fonder and fonder of you.'"

I didn't find Na Yeong-gyu unpleasant, but his life plan was a stumbling block I kept tripping over, and it kept me from feeling at ease when I met him. Besides, he was anxious to fulfill the plans he made as fast as he could. Countless marriage preparations were waiting for him: the two families had to meet, the date had to be fixed, the honeymoon had to be planned, an apartment had to be found. So much to do! He was waiting for a definite answer from me—not just an answer, but a definite answer. As soon as he had it, he was going to dash off to set his perfect, elaborate wedding plans into motion. I asked him to wait.

"How long?" His response was immediate. I hesitated, since I thought he deserved more precise information to help him with his life planning.

"About three months."

"That long?"

"That won't have any real effect on your plan to get married when you're twenty-nine."

"Still, that's too long. Make it one month."

I didn't answer. One month, three months. That wasn't the issue. I just had no way of knowing what would help me decide whether to marry him or not.

I was really curious. It didn't matter if it was Na Yeong-gyu or Kim Jang-u or somebody else. How and when would I be able to make up my mind and say, "Yes, I will marry him"? How did all those people who are married decide, anyway?

矛
盾

8 Sweet Ju-ri

Life
Sometimes makes us choose evil
Willingly,
Inevitably.
We have to live hand in hand
*   with contradiction.*
Can't Ju-ri sense this at all?

It had never crossed my mind that Ju-ri might visit our house. To be honest, she'd been buried in a distant corner of my memories since I saw her at Auntie's last month, partly because I was preoccupied with so many other things, but even if I hadn't been, I had no particular reason to think of her.

One day, out of the blue, she knocked at our gate as I was finishing washing up after arriving home from work. I opened the gate, still drying my face with a towel. Ju-ri stood there, with a smile that was hard to read.

"I was passing by, so I thought I'd drop in."

That was her excuse—just dropping by her aunt's since she was in the neighborhood. She'd never visited once since she had matured, and here it was past 7 p.m., time for her to be heading back home even if she'd been out. Of course I didn't believe her. First of all, I found it pretty suspicious that she knew where we lived well enough to just drop in. We've moved at least five times since she began studying in the U.S., and we hadn't even been in this house six months. My aunt, though, my sweet aunt, would visit us at least once, no matter where we had moved.

My aunt must have been driving somewhere in the neighborhood and realized that I'd be the only one home. She must want Ju-ri and me to get close. I bet she dragged her daughter up to the gate and then shushed her and snuck out of the alley when she heard me coming out. She would have cast a final glance towards our house and smiled gently, before getting back in her car and blending into the darkening streets. That's Auntie.

I brought Ju-ri to my room. There was nowhere else in our house I could have welcomed her. I wasn't embarrassed to show her our shabby little home, but it did make me very uncomfortable that we simply had no place where Ju-ri and I could sit across from each other and talk without feeling awkward.

"It's strange for me to see a room without a bed. Is there a reason you don't like them?"

Ju-ri scanned the room for something to sit on. When she saw that I only had a desk chair, she realized she had no choice but to sit on the floor. Her question suggested there was something strange. Why don't I like beds? I interpreted her words as an expression of concern, that I might be so ashamed of my tiny room that I hadn't put a bed in it. Ju-ri was a talented young woman who would soon receive her doctorate. For her to talk as she did about poverty must have stemmed from her Ph.D.-to-be's intellect.

"It's too crowded back here, and people are unfriendly. Why do they stare so much? It's not right. It's rude. Today I went out shopping with my mom and now I'm just plain exhausted."

She stretched her legs and leaned back against the wall. Her bare calves, slender and pale, showed beneath her short skirt. Her toes were small and tender, her heels round and pink, and her ankles bulged delicately, like a glass sculpture. Such pretty feet, and here they had just suffered their greatest hardship in her whole life after a day's worth of hard shopping. Unconsciously my eyes were drawn to a pair of socks hanging on a clothesline in the yard. I wanted to get them and hide my own bare feet inside them. I take after my father as far as my hands and feet go; they're disproportionately large.

I didn't want to be reminded of my father in front of Ju-ri—I wanted to hide everything that might make her think of him. I wondered if she remembered what she said to me once long ago.

"Your dad is like King Kong."

The four cousins—Ju-ri, Ju-hyeok, Jin-mo and I—were watching a video of *King Kong* that my aunt had rented for us. Suddenly Ju-ri looked back at me and made that declaration. King Kong, dark, huge, hideous, was trampling a city, his nose twitching. I trembled in terror as I watched the screen, but Ju-ri's words were as terrifying as Kong himself.

"I mean it. He's like bad King Kong."

I had no answer. Saying it once was not enough—she had to repeat it to drive the point home.

Jin-mo's eyes pleaded with me to teach Ju-ri a lesson for talking like that. I had to turn away. I felt terrible. I just bit my lips and muttered to myself, "If I were her, I wouldn't say such a thing... I wouldn't say such a thing to cousins who had to hide here..."

"Have you had dinner?" I hadn't eaten yet, but I wanted to avoid having to chew my rice with Ju-ri when we didn't have any side dishes to put on the table with it. I thought I'd hate Auntie for bringing Ju-ri around now, if the two of us had to eat together.

"Yeah, don't worry about it. Mom and I ate together before six, and I won't eat anything else until tomorrow. We're dieting these days."

I was reminded again how thoughtful and considerate my aunt is. We think alike about things and have the same tastes. But Auntie is not my mother. She's Ju-ri's mother.

"I hear you're working. Are you going to leave school? You can always work later on, but it's hard to catch up if you miss out on your chance to study. Mom is worried too. She said she can pay your tuition, but you're stubborn."

She tilted her head slightly and gazed at me. I merely smiled back. Her expression was exactly like my aunt's. I remembered that Ju-ri had been a tender, sweet child, even if she did sometimes unwittingly scratch my heart with thoughtless words. From childhood she's never caused her mother any pain, unlike me. I was curt with my mother and ran away from home at a moment's notice to join my bored friends. I talked back and defied her constantly. Ju-ri was an angel sent from heaven compared to me.

"I'm really sorry about Jin-mo. But what he did wasn't right. People shouldn't do things like that. I really don't know—I have trouble understanding why he lives the way he does."

Her angelic face was stern as she criticized his behaviour. She was right. Obviously he shouldn't be gathering thugs to beat a rival over the back of the head with a stick. But I wouldn't talk like that. Doesn't she realize that life can't be explained that simply? Life sometimes makes us choose evil willingly, inevitably. We have to live hand in hand with contradiction. Can't Ju-ri sense this at all?

I had no answer for Ju-ri this time either. What she was saying was very difficult for me because I couldn't simply agree, but I did my best with her. I was genuinely trying to find common ground with this cousin of mine who was visiting me with such earnestness after so long, and I said, "What happened woke Jin-mo up. He's not going to waste his life anymore. I'm sorry we worried you all so much."

Mom needed money to buy off the man Jin-mo beat up in order to get a deposition from him that would lighten Jin-mo's sentence. My aunt had supplied some of it, and I had no doubt that my mother's prickly sense of self-respect would force her to pay it back. Even so, Auntie was the only person to lend us money immediately, without a word of complaint. Ju-ri wouldn't know about that, though. The ugly happenings of our house were the only things my aunt had to feel ashamed about in front of her husband and children.

"Don't talk like that. You make it sound like we're not family. I'm just saying all this because I feel sorry for you and Jin-mo. Well, let's change the subject. How are you these days, anyway? Do you have a boyfriend?"

"What about you? Are you seeing anybody in America?" I realized that one way to make the conversation work would be to return the question I had just received, so I volleyed it back at her.

"Yes, but it's too early to think about getting married. I have to finish my degree first. And you?"

"Well, there is somebody I love, but of course I'm still trying to decide whether to marry him or not." The answer slipped out of my mouth before I even knew what I was saying. Somebody I love? Who do I mean?

"You should get married if you're in love. What are you waiting for?" Ju-ri's eyes widened. I felt stifled again, and that made me angry inside.

"Do people get married just because they love each other? There are lots of issues to consider. Marriage is business, a crucial business in our lives."

"Business? Did you just call marriage a 'business'?"

Ju-ri practically jumped up in shock. As I looked at her, it dawned on me that conversation with her called for the secret formula of my mother's hyperbole.

"You really shouldn't think like that. I mean, it's not right. Marriage isn't business. It's a beautiful blessing in which pure love meets pure love. Am I wrong?"

"Yes, you're wrong."

Her jaw dropped. She looked as dumbfounded as though she were talking to somebody who insisted on calling soybeans red beans.

"Have you heard the saying that marriage is a twenty-year jail term for women and lifelong probation for men? Well, shouldn't we make our sentence as light as possible? That's what I think. The smartest thing is to weigh everything up very carefully and then choose the sentence that's easiest to bear."

"Why do you think like that, Jin-jin? Is everyone here like you? They don't care about love and treat marriage like a business deal?"

"What's wrong with business deals? What's bad is businessmen who lie or cheat."

I was on the verge of making some cutting remark about "people here" and "people over there" but I restrained myself, recalling once again that Ju-ri is a nice kid. She was unable to erase an expression that said she'd finally seen my true colors. Once more she cried out, "Oh, that's not right."

That little exclamation seemed to have become her favorite phrase since she arrived at our house.

"You interpret the world in black and white, but it's not like that. We live in a world where most things are in shades of grey. I don't know if what you're studying is that uncomplicated, but my life has not been. I'm not ready to make any conclusions."

"I think what you're saying about shades of gray is a cop-out. It sounds like you're trying to be clever. If that's the way the world is, why bother to try to do our best in this life? Why do we call love a miracle? Now I feel really depressed. I didn't know you were like that. Maybe you're . . ."

Ju-ri trailed off, unable to continue. She just kept looking at me quietly, a sad expression on her face. I was waiting. I already knew what she was going to say, but nothing she said could hurt me anymore.

"Maybe you . . . you were influenced a lot by your dad. I understand. It's your father who made you like this . . ."

As I expected. Ju-ri was telling me she could just barely begin to understand me if she thought of my father—a drunk, a bum, a madman. Maybe my father made me the way I am now. I don't know. But it wasn't fair to make him the explanation for things turning out badly, as Ju-ri was doing. Maybe I could explain Dad to her just once. At any rate, she was the kind-hearted daughter of my aunt, and I was very fond of Auntie. I had to keep trying.

"My dad taught me how to think. What proof do we have that we've lived other than the thoughts in our heads? He taught me an important truth. We need to think deeply about what goes on in our lives. If he did anything wrong, it's that he thought too much and went beyond what he was capable of. That's another lesson he left me—it's painful to go beyond your limits. He taught me something other fathers couldn't teach in their whole lives. He fulfilled all his duties to his children with that alone."

Ju-ri was quiet. Her silence was asking whether I really forgave my father, the drunk, the bum, the madman. I was happy to answer.

"My father made my life richer. I love him."

"Your father . . ."

Ju-ri finally began to talk. She cleared her throat briefly after the words "your father," and continued quickly, avoiding my eyes, " . . . ignored his responsibilities to his family. That's not right. You can't rationalize it away. Otherwise, why do so many fathers support their families? Is the way they're living wrong? What's wrong is always wrong. I don't understand why I should have to keep explaining that."

There it was again, her favorite phrase. She simply remained in hiding behind this expression and refused to come out into the world. Ju-ri hadn't matured at all since she compared my father to King Kong as a child. I decided to let my understanding of Ju-ri go this far and no further—there are people in this world who have no interest in exploring the many mysteries that life holds. Perhaps that itself is another of life's interesting mysteries.

That day I keenly realized that I can no longer say anything about my cousins. The passage of time has opened a wide gulf between us but done nothing to bridge it.

Ju-ri was unable to erase her sad expression before returning home that day. After she left, my mood wasn't exactly cheerful either. Intuition told me I might never be able to fulfil my aunt's wish that Ju-ri and I get closer. If it weren't for Auntie, I'd hope never to see Ju-ri again.

Ju-ri must have confessed a similar premonition to her mother, because the next day Auntie called me at work.

"Did Ju-ri say something harsh? I don't think of her like that, but . . ." Her voice was sad.

"No, Auntie. We had a long, helpful talk and then she left. Did she say I upset her?"

I played dumb for Auntie's sake. Ju-ri would clearly think this kind of lie is "not right," but I'm me and not her, and I can act the way I want.

"Jin-jin, give her a break. You do that for me, don't you? What else has she done so far but study? Oh, she and Ju-hyeok are going back tomorrow. I really hate those first few days after they go back. I can't get used to home without them. Silly, isn't it? It's been almost ten years, but it's always just as hard as it was the first time."

I told her what Ju-ri and I talked about the previous day to console her, editing it to make it all sound pretty. I didn't hesitate to distort the parts that didn't fit together smoothly. She listened happily to what I told her. I could tell she was censoring and distorting her feelings as well. As she was hanging up, she suddenly called my name in a serious voice.

"Jin-jin . . ."

"Yes? What?"

"Jin-jin, I'm sorry. They're my own flesh and blood—I love them more than I love you . . . I'm really sorry."

Truly, that's the sort of person my aunt was. She probably didn't know that her last remark made me burst into tears. I hung up quickly to hide them, as they welled up and tumbled down my cheeks. Wiping them away with the back of my hand, I looked out the window.

Summer was passing into autumn. The sky, high and blue, gazed down upon the world with indifference.

矛盾

9 On the Road to Dosol Hermitage, Seonun Temple

*T*he only thing that can ease unhappiness
Is another's unhappiness.
That's human nature.
Conquering unhappiness is surprisingly
    easy
As long as you don't think
You've been wronged.
Nothing heals a wound
But a wound.

I've already mentioned I can handle liquor. If I have a special talent, it's my ability to drink—I hold my own against most men who can put it away, never mind women.

I had no real chance to test my limit until I started attending university. I just found the drunks who staggered and passed out in the street late at night very odd. From my experience it seemed that I'd have to drink a virtually endless amount for that to happen. After all, who can measure how much water there is in the ocean?

At college, I began to hear lots of information about how much other people could drink in terms of numbers: "Last night I passed out after two bottles of *soju*." "The three of us finished off a whole tub's worth of *makkeolli*." "There's a guy in Phys. Ed. who can go to a Chinese restaurant, down two bowls of *kaoliang* in a row and stay sober."[1] It was only once I had some numbers from other people to go by that I could confirm just how much of Dad's amazing capacity I had inherited.

I never turned down a drink when I was at university; I never got to the point of tottering around or collapsing either. Still, I've never been so foolish as to test just how much I could handle, and I never envied the stories guys told of their heroic drinking exploits, how they drank until they passed out. Once you master something or really excel at it, things get dull. You just yawn and roll over. You become as blasé as the ocean is about the streams that flow into it. That was my attitude towards drinking.

I definitely take after my father in keeping my sense of coordination no matter how much I drink. If Dad didn't say himself how many bottles of *soju* he had had, nobody could tell how much he had drank—or practically whether he'd even been drinking at all. Long before he lost his sense of balance, he

---

1. *Makkeoli* is a traditional fermented Korean liquor made out of rice of relatively low alcohol content, while *kaoliang* is Chinese and sorghum-based.

would lose his mental equilibrium and snap. That was his curse. Except at the very beginning of my university days, when I first realized I could drink other people under the table, I never tried to down as much as I could. Fear of something similar happening held me back. I didn't want to lose control in front of other people. I had absolutely no interest in tasting a moment of complete abandon. Even if my father failed, I have to live my life with self-control, no matter what it takes.

I have a confession to make, though. Enough of dropping hints with all this boring talk about drinking. Let me spit out the truth. It can happen to me too. I finally lost control.

Rain had been falling all day long and sweeping the debris of autumn away towards the ocean—maple leaves ablaze with red, worm-eaten oak leaves, wildflowers that had passed their bloom and now lay strewn about.[2] It wasn't Seoul. And I wasn't alone. Kim Jang-u was by my side.

We postponed the autumn trip we had planned for September, because the weather refused to cooperate. No matter how long we waited, it did not seem like autumn, and so the trip wound up being put off quite naturally until October. Several other reasons had come up as well. First of all, Jang-u had to stand by helplessly as his brother's travel agency crumbled. His brother sold off everything—his apartment, land he'd set aside in the country so he and Jang-u might live next to each other when they got old, even his car. Jang-u turned over to his brother all the money he'd been saving in installments, down to a passbook with just a few hundred thousand won in it. His brother just took the passbook with the few hundred thousand won. Returning the rest, he patted Jang-u on the back and said, "Hey pal, you should leave at least a little seed money if you don't want to starve to death . . ."

I was having a tough time too. I had Jin-mo, who was waiting to stand trial, to worry about. Mom never got around to opening up her shop. She was too busy going over the information from the prosecutor's office. Her spirit was a little broken after she lost a chunk of cash to a swindler who suckered people into thinking he'd take care of things with the authorities. Nevertheless, her routine never changed. She got up every morning, full of energy, like a toy doll whose batteries are replaced daily. She bustled around all day long until she ran out of juice in the evening.

She amazed me. After getting fleeced by that con artist, she ran straight off to the bookstore and came back with a volume on criminal law. She reasoned that she could win a lawsuit only if she knew the law—completely sound

---

2. Attentive readers will note later that there is a discrepancy between the text here and the description of the weather on the day when Jin-jin in fact loses control. In personal communication Yang Gui-ja remarks that she plans to amend the passage above in later editions of the book.

logic. The only issue was whether she'd be able to read a book for specialists. I went downtown to rummage through a large bookstore and found two books on law for her written in an easy style, one by an ex-prosecutor and the other by a practising lawyer.

Late into the night, my mother, wearing reading glasses, pored over these stories from law courts on behalf of Jin-mo. Like I said, she turns to books whenever she is boxed into a corner. A few months ago it was Japanese conversation. Now it was criminal law. Come to think of it, she's had to read other books just as abstruse when she's tried to cope with unexpected crises. I don't remember the exact title, but there was one medical text called something like *Understanding and Treating Schizophrenia*. She had picked it out because of Dad, and it was thick enough for her to use as a pillow when she fell asleep in the middle of reading it. She tried to read these latest books seriously, just like she used to. Actually, she looked much more serious now than she had back then, before she had the spectacles. They made her reading seem much more convincing.

This won't be the last time Mom will have to wade through a text. I have no idea what difficult topic she'll need to sift through next time to carry on her fight against the world, but one thing is obvious: she won't be buying the novels and poetry collections Auntie reads. As twins, they share a tendency to rely on books, but the ones they choose are exact opposites. Just like their lives.

My mother was frenzied in her activity on Jin-mo's behalf. And me? All I did was visit him once. Seeing him in a prison uniform that one time was enough. I made up my mind not to put my name down on the prison's visit request form again. Jin-mo and I felt exactly the same about this.

"Sis, don't come. It's one thing for Mom to visit, but I don't want you to be coming back and forth here. Got it?" He raised his voice with that final question and frowned. "It's okay here. It's easier to put up with than I thought. Worth checking out at least once, but not worth sticking around long."

If you get through a difficult situation, you wind up proud of yourself, no matter what it is you've accomplished—even if it's committing a crime and going to prison. Jin-mo had gotten himself back on his high horse, and his expression showed he'd already grasped how to play his role. This time he'd chosen to act the part of a master criminal on death row.

I'm going have to toss away the hope that Jin-mo will turn over a new leaf. He's not like the people kids read about in schoolbooks. Maybe he believes he can start again, but his life never changes. The only thing that changes for him are the roles he plays. He can play any part handed to him, as long as he has an idol to model himself on.

I never cried because of Jin-mo, but Jang-u wept in front of me because of his own brother. It was the first time I felt sorry I hadn't told him about what was going on with Jin-mo. Words are no comfort to the broken-hearted. The most effective way to console someone in pain is to share pain of your own. "Is that what you're upset over? I've had to deal with the same thing. Maybe what happened to me was even worse. Compared to me, you're lucky . . ."

The only thing that can ease unhappiness is another's unhappiness. That's human nature.

Conquering unhappiness is surprisingly easy as long as you don't think you've been wronged. If I could have told Jang-u that my only brother was wearing a prison uniform while waiting to stand trial, it would have gone a long way toward relieving his own pain. I hesitated several times, but decided not to say anything in the end. It wasn't until our trip that I understood why I didn't and why I find it so difficult to show him who I really am.

But I realized why when we were on our way back and I recognized my true self at last. I'm not ready yet to say what I learned, though. I think I should still be more suspicious of it all. I have to consider the consequences of everything that's going on more fully.

I was the one who set the date for our trip. Nothing strange about that—that's how it always was with Jang-u. I first applied for three days' leave from work and then told him what I'd done.

"Is that okay?"

I wasn't certain what he meant but I said yes.

"Are you sure?" This time I could tell he definitely wasn't asking about external issues like work or home. Yes, I said once again. But then I wondered, "Okay up to what point? . . ."

Are you okay?

Jang-u asked me once more not just as we set off, but again and again during our three-day trip.

"I'd like to head to Mt. Dosol and go to Seonun Temple. The drive from Buan along the ocean is nice. Is that okay?"

"Wherever you want to go is fine with me."

That's how we decided where we were going. We had set the date for departure, and at that point all we had to do was leave and drift with the wind. Follow the clouds. Jang-u was not Yeong-gyu. I didn't expect a detailed itinerary. I was amazed he'd even gone so far as suggesting Seonun Temple as a destination. Even more amazing, when he showed up at the time we had arranged, his jeep was so clean I hardly recognized it. He was obviously preparing for the trip in his own way. I smiled in spite of myself, because it was clear he'd spent all day polishing and waxing his car. He is very awkward at showing what he has in his heart, but the emotions are all there.

Chapter 9 On the Road to Dosol Hermitage, Seonun Temple

"An Jin-jin! Are you okay?"

He asked the question once an hour, his expression tense, between Seoul and Gochang. Including lunch, the drive took five hours, but he asked the question as if he'd still turn around and drive home then and there if I said no. Maybe that was why some tragic resolve I didn't understand was slowly taking shape inside me. I felt I was travelling on a predestined path that I could not turn back from.

But it wasn't just that. The road ran along the coast, past waves, blue-green, endlessly sparkling. The landscape was so magnificent that it evoked tears, exuded a breathtaking, tragic beauty. We rode in silence. The jeep can roll off into the sea . . . I wouldn't mind . . . just become part of the surf . . . leave this wearying life behind . . . it doesn't matter . . . it's really okay . . .

But fields of red earth reappeared, and farming villages passed by one by one. I kept turning around, unable to forget the ocean. Everything in the world that we can't forget always lies behind us. Maybe that's why. Maybe that's why we can't abandon the past.

The sky was beginning to glow crimson with sunset when we arrived at Mt. Seonun and parked. The hotels, bars, and restaurants had already illuminated their green and red neon signs. It was high season, and it was crowded with tourists here too. Jang-u, uncertain, hadn't budged from the driver's seat. I would have to take the lead again.

"See that motel? That's where I want to stay. Let's head over there. That's okay, isn't it?" I didn't hesitate to avail myself of his question.

"If it's okay with you, I . . ."

And so our lodging for the next two nights was decided.

The motel had the look of a simple villa. Its outer wall was adorned with stones and each room had a small balcony attached to it. As expected I was in charge of getting our room. I'd never intended or even wanted to consider separate rooms, but there were so many guests it was out of the question. I always laughed with scorn whenever I came across couples like that in novels or movies. Everybody knows they do what they want whether they take one room or two.

Fortunately the room was set up to sleep in traditional style on the *ondol* floor.[3] The mere thought of lying with Jang-u in a Western bed horrified me. I had no confidence I could cope with the various images a bed would conjure up for us. Images guide our emotions, not the other way around. I didn't think I'd be able to stand my shame. City life, in its worldliness, has taught us that what beds require is flesh not souls. Especially hotel beds.

---

3. *Ondol* is the traditional Korean heating system in which the floor is warmed from underneath by heated flues. Now heated water pipes tend to be used.

The first night was very straightforward, and we observed faithfully the warning about beds. We ate dinner, went for a walk, bought two bottles of beer, returned to our room, drank one apiece, took turns showering, laid out two sleeping mats side by side, and fell asleep. Just like an elderly couple on a trip to a hot spring. I checked the clock before going to sleep. 11:05. God, I hardly ever went to bed this early even at home.

"What are you so afraid of that we have to go to bed so soon?" I piped up finally, as I switched off the light.

"Nothing. I'm just tired from driving." He grinned and, pretending to be exhausted, turned over. And that was all. I slept well. I don't know about Jang-u. At some point, in the middle of the night or early in the morning, I heard the balcony door slide open. I never heard it close again.

It wasn't until the next day that I realized he wasn't lugging around his huge, aging bag stuffed with cameras, lenses and film.

We looked around Seonun Temple and headed up the valley toward Dosol Hermitage. Every time he stopped, wild flowers reminded me of the camera he had left behind.

"This is a *maeminamul*.[4] It blooms and then it wilts, all alone in the forest. It's wrong to cut its stem, because it feels pain and bleeds." The yellow flower barely clung to its stem. I felt tender towards it.

"The real name of this one is *gujeolcho*, but it usually gets called a wild chrysanthemum. People call certain species of aster or flowers like *gamguk* or *sanguk* wild chrysanthemums too, but that's not showing them proper respect. If you love flowers, then of course you should call them by their real names, and frequently at that. How can something be true love if you don't have the name right?"

"Why didn't you bring your camera?"

Even without his camera, Jang-u spent a long time by the flowers, unable to leave them, as he moved from side to side and tried to frame them in a proper composition.

"If I had it with me I'd just take pictures, instead of really seeing them."

"That makes sense."

"There's another reason too, Jin-jin. You're with me. Why bring my camera when you're here beside me to talk to me, to laugh with me, when I can hear the sound of your breathing? Every moment is full. I decided that on this trip

---

4. Botanical name: *Hylomecon vernale maxim*. The Korean name may be taken literally as "cicada herb." The plant is also known as *pinamul* or "blood herb." The botanical names of the plants mentioned in the following paragraph are *chrysanthemum sibiricum* (Kor. *gujeolcho*), *chrysanthemum indicum* (Kor. *gamguk*), and *chrysanthemum boreale makino* (Kor. *sanguk*), respectively.

I'd concentrate on saying your name, Jin-jin, rather than the names of my beloved flowers."

I really liked that he could say such things. Instead of answering, I held his hand.

"It still doesn't seem real to me. Tonight you'll fall asleep breathing peacefully beside me, just like last night. It's only just dawning on me that there could be days like this in my life. I never even knew it was possible and used to just think about how lonely I was. But I've decided not to have those negative thoughts anymore. Can I? That's okay, isn't it?"

But I said nothing. I didn't tell him it was okay. I just narrowed the distance between us as we walked along the wooded path side by side. Since our shoulders were touching it was difficult to hold hands. But Jang-u did what he ought to at that moment and, shifting his position, put his arm around me. I leaned against him as we walked along that fragrant forest path. To be honest, though, it didn't seem real to me yet either. Was this love? Was it love to walk leaning against each other like that?

Kim Jang-u definitely possessed qualities Na Yeong-gyu lacked. A date with Yeong-gyu meant a collision with reality, but time spent with Jang-u was a dream, and the dream that is love holds within it a temptation to run away from reality. I felt . . . I felt something that made me want to run and run until I couldn't run anymore, something that made me think I couldn't stop running even if I crashed and shattered, something sublime that would have made it all right even if I shattered and died. If what made me feel all those things is love, then I felt love for the very first time that day as we walked to Dosol Hermitage.

But after being aware of love within myself for the first time on that path, I suddenly felt sluggish. It was strange. Nothing had happened—all I had done was ask myself "Is this love?" and answered yes.

And even though that was all that had taken place, I gradually grew depressed. I couldn't walk straight or focus properly. A gaping hole appeared in my heart that allowed autumn's chill air to pass in and out.

I was confused. Anybody would have been confused. I've never heard anyone own up to feeling what love made me feel. I flatter myself that I've read a lot of books, having inherited Mom and Auntie's fondness for them. And I may not be a movie fanatic, but I've seen my share, for one reason or another. Were all those books and films lying? If not, something must have been wrong with me to feel so desolate.

Confusion turns me into an utter wreck—it's my weakness. I gradually began to spoil the second day of the trip. There were signs I was headed for trouble. First of all, it was odd that scenes of the West Sea from the previous day kept popping into my head.

"Are you okay, An Jin-jin? You don't look right. If you're not feeling well, let's just go back to the room and rest. It's okay with me."

He looked at me blankly, as I turned down his suggestion that we have lunch first and headed to the parking lot and his jeep.

"We can have lunch by the ocean if we get hungry. There's still lots of time. Let's get out of here."

God, that was abrupt of me to say we had lots of time. Time to do what? The words shot out of my mouth before I even knew what I was saying. I can't stand it when I act like that. Jang-u, knowing full well he's not very good at filling up spare moments, started the car, looking apologetic.

"I've got a headache." I leaned back against the seat, and he put his hand against my forehead. I closed my eyes without thinking. Another mistake. Closed my eyes? So childish of me. But I wasn't brave enough to keep my eyes open and watch his face come closer.

"You've got a temperature. What should we do?"

His breath rushed out over my face. His hand still rested on my forehead, and he was mumbling. We both knew our first kiss had taken place in his old jeep. I hated that I knew it. I'm not naive. I'm not all fuzzy. I hated how my mind stayed clear even as my forehead burned hot.

And then, of all moments, as I was feeling disgusted with myself for having all these thoughts and not giving myself up to love, his hands moved. He started to stroke my cheeks hesitantly, and touched my nose and lips. My breath came with great difficulty and suddenly I became afraid. Too clever for my own good. I knew what he was going to do next and what he was going to say. I hated pretending not to know. My thoughts, settling into a deep abyss, urged me not to tease him. Open your eyes wide. But I was too late. His face, enormous, filled my field of vision, and he spoke.

"I love you."

I stared straight into his eyes. I saw myself reflected in the black pupils that were suddenly exposed in my gaze. They trembled. I looked away quickly, and his hands went back to their original position. Really lucky, I thought, that his jeep was in a corner of the parking lot. I guessed that he'd also become concerned about prying eyes and done no more than rest his hand on my forehead. Such were my thoughts as I sat next to the man who had just said, "I love you." We remained like that for a long time. I looked outside; he looked at me.

Our positions were frozen "that afternoon," me looking out the window and Jang-u stealing occasional glances at me. My stubbornness in continuing to stare out the window eventually made his expression stiffen as well. But I had no control over what I was doing. Ever since I had decided, "Ah, this is love," I couldn't help it. I wanted to know when he had decided he loved me too and to ask him what he had felt when he realized it. Did he feel the way I did—that somebody was grabbing him, tugging at his ankles? That a hole had formed in his heart? Did he feel a loneliness so deep that it made him want to cry?

The ocean was just as beautiful the second time around. Fishing boats bobbed on the water, with little pieces of friendly cumulus clouds tailing after them. Blue water rippled in fine, delicate patterns beneath the steep cliffs.

The window was wide open. I propped my chin in my hand against it and stared out at the sea. Could it really be true that typhoons sometimes blow over that quiet ocean? Seagulls flew among autumn sunbeams broken up by the waves. It made perfect sense for seagulls to be living there, but they caught me off guard. I couldn't give myself up to love, but the sea was beautiful enough for me to devote my entire spirit to it.

They say love is beautiful. Lies. All lies. Love was not as beautiful as the ocean. But love was still love, and even though it wasn't beautiful, the hollow feeling that had settled upon me was clearly love. Because of this man beside me, driving along this road with its tortuous curves and wearing a stiff expression on his face, I'd experienced love for the first time. I'll learn what it's like to be in love through this man who must have asked silently at least a dozen times by now, "An Jin-jin, are you okay?" Love. Sometimes ugly, sometimes sad and sometimes beautiful . . .

We drove that stretch of road between Buan and Gochang six times that day, believe it or not.

"Please, just once more."

As soon as we headed inland again from the coast, I grew anxious. He turned the car around on a side road without a word, and we went back in the direction we had come.

"Again. Faster this time."

Jang-u complied obediently. After a certain point, a lit cigarette never left his hand. His jeep, incapable of high speeds, sputtered along the coast road, making rude noises. The only time Jang-u needed to slow down was when we came to blind corners. My hair fluttered wildly in the wind off the ocean, but I never grew tired of the sea. My worry was that I might grow tired of it. I had a premonition that if I got out of the car and went to sit somewhere I'd collapse. That feeling bound me to the sea.

But we couldn't ride forever. What good is a car that can only move forward without stopping? Life is the same. You have to stop sometimes. I finally called it quits after the sixth lap, once it dawned on me that if the water of the ocean couldn't plug the hole in my heart, liquor might do the trick. The idea was just comforting enough to allow me to put an end to our laps on the course. I wasn't entirely free from worries about alcohol turning our remaining time into a shambles, but I was confident for the most part. I'd never been bested by liquor before, not me, not An Jin-jin. A tragic sense that it was finally time to have my showdown with destiny suddenly created an intense thirst within me.

"I'm so thirsty I can't even talk," I said as we sat down. We had come to a restaurant in Gyeokpo that specialized in sashimi.

"Please get us a Coke or Sprite right away."

"And a bottle of *soju*."

In a parched voice I added one more item to Jang-u's order. He looked at me. His hair had become tangled in the wind, and it made him appear exhausted. I avoided his gaze and looked out on the expanse of ocean. Men were walking along the sandy beach, their pant legs rolled up. They were accompanied by women who were hoisting the edge of their skirts and laughing loudly.

At first I hadn't at all intended to drink recklessly. A showdown with destiny requires preparation, so I was planning on a decent meal before I attacked the *soju*. Even if I was going to go overboard, I wasn't going to be so dumb as to drink on an empty stomach. But that's not what happened.

One shot of *soju* did nothing to quench my parching thirst. It wasn't until my fifth that I felt I could breathe easily. We already had plenty of side dishes on the table even before the sashimi came out, but I had no appetite. I trusted myself, having been through this many times before. I could drink several bottles before going home and then, feeling completely sober, get a dinner together and empty a bowl of rice without problem. But a few shots of *soju* stirred up an arrogance inside me.

And so it began. I didn't have a single spoonful of rice, just a few sashimi slices at Jang-u's urging. At some point he stopped ordering more bottles for me, so I had to take care of it myself. Up until then I had not been the slightest bit drunk. Since we were the only customers I had to flag down the owner myself to order more *soju*. She was outside attending to some other business, and I paid for all the food we had so far and went back inside. My memory is clear until that point. I also remember giving myself a solemn warning not to forget Jang-u's dire financial state no matter how much I drank. Come on. Forget about that. Stop. Just try to drink, drink . . . drink . . . please, just drink.

"Enough. Come on. Stop. Are you okay?"

How many times did he cry out? Ten, twenty?

"Can you please stop with the 'Are you okay'? Don't you have anything original to say?"

How many times did I shout that back at him? Three, four, a half dozen?

Then a few more words "Let's go back. I want to drink too, but I'm driving. Let's go back and then we can both drink all we want." He was trying to calm me down. I think I answered yes, because that sounded tempting, but . . .

Right after that something finally happened that I still find hard to believe—the scenes in my head begin to get patchy. Everything is a mess after that point. The memories cut out, return, cut out, return and then are gone completely. I'd never had gaps in my memory before, let alone a complete blackout. Later, when I realised what had happened, I was shocked.

I vaguely remember having whiskey in a nightclub next to our motel when we went back. Even in the midst of it all, I think I was still worrying about his pathetic wallet.

"*Soju*. I want *soju*. It's not good to mix . . ."

Jang-u tells me that's what I said.

"Why is everything so strange, Jang-u? All of a sudden I don't know how to live in this world. I'm afraid. I've forgotten how to live. Is this what happens when you're in love? Does love make the world so strange? . . ."

I don't remember saying anything about the *soju*, but I do have a hazy memory of my desperate confession, probably because I had spoken from the heart. There was nothing to add or subtract. That afternoon I was overwhelmed with a sense of desperation, like a long distance runner who suddenly forgets how to run at the starting line of a race. Right foot first? Or left foot? Is that even how you're supposed to propel your body forward? Jang-u would never know that feeling—the despair of the marathon runner who had suddenly forgotten everything was all mine.

How did we get back here?

That was the first question in my head when I woke up in our room the next morning. I opened my eyes and greeted the morning, lying on the same mat as the previous day. Kim Jang-u lay sleeping deeply on a mat beside me. He looked exhausted. His face was turned towards me and he had one arm tossed across the floor. It made him seem lonesome, like a man who had tried to catch something but missed.

The next thing I noticed was my clothes. I had very definitely been wearing blue jeans and a sweater last night, but now I had on the shorts and plain T-shirt I had brought to sleep in and worn the first night as well. When my thoughts reached that point I jumped up from the sleeping mat. I don't remember changing clothes, I don't remember that at all. With that silent realization, I flopped back down on the bedding. As I lay there prone, a few memories sank in. I clutched frantically at each one, trying to put the jigsaw puzzle of what had happened back together.

Jang-u, wiping my face with a wet towel. It must have been in the room . . . me vomiting, terrified by something . . . no, not just wiping my face . . . my feet, the nape of my neck, a cold towel rubbing my chest . . .

And . . . and . . . Jang-u taking off my clothes. I think I asked him to do it, but the details . . . his face coming closer, looking furious . . . I saw his naked chest, his collarbone protruding. . . Then, something that had been waiting to happen happened. . . Only then did my mind relax into sleep . . . I've fulfilled everything at last . . . I was at peace.

Once I had pieced together my memories up to that point, I stretched and turned to lie more comfortably. I could calm down now. I knew what I had done. It's okay to sleep a bit, I thought. I sensed I had done everything I could, and I wanted to enjoy peace now.

I turned to the left. Jang-u slept soundly, his face free of care; he felt to me like my own flesh and blood. I softly stroked his arm, which looked so lonely stretched out on the floor. I felt my love spilling over, like water spilling over a pot, and unconsciously I buried my face against his arm. A few moments later his arm signalled that he was stirring from sleep.

"Are you okay?" A peaceful voice. I nodded. "A drinker. A real drinker." He pulled me into his arms and sighed. "Why did you do it?"

"Do what?" I asked cautiously. I couldn't bear to say I had blacked out. Had I done something else?

"Down in the club. You hit me. Don't you remember? You slapped my face and punched me all over my back. You shouted, 'Don't lock me up. I'm afraid. I'll die if you lock me up.' I felt terrible to think I'd caused you so much pain. . . Let me ask you something. Am I a prison to you?"

Prison? As in prison guard? Did I say that?

I shuddered. That was my father's monologue. The first night my father ran amok, he kept saying, "You were like a prison guard locking me up. You don't know how terrifying that sense of despair is . . ."

My father was within me. My missing father lived inside me. I dug myself deeper into Jang-u's arms to hide my trembling.

"Answer me. Do you think I'll be like a prison to you?"

"No. Never. What I meant . . . what I meant was I'm afraid I might love you too much. It's true. That's what I genuinely feel."

"Really?"

"Yes. Yesterday was the first time I realized for sure that I've fallen in love. It was hard for me to deal with. It's hard . . . to be in love."

Just as I swore to him again and again, I meant every word I said. Just as my father meant every word he said to my mother after he sobered up the next day and begged for forgiveness.

Chapter 9 On the Road to Dosol Hermitage, Seonun Temple

That morning I finally understood that my father loved my mother very much and that because of his love for her, his love for Jin-mo and me was absolute. His boundless love for us trapped him behind an iron door, three layers thick. It was only to be expected that he struggled for so long, dreaming of escape.

矛盾

10 Three Memos about Love

Love is a red light.
 When it's lit you have to stop.
 It warns of danger and promises safety.
 A red light.
 That's love.

Love
    Means not feeling completely free in front of an unused telephone, no matter where you are—at home, at work, or on the street. Telephones cage you more tenaciously than an occupying army. For someone who has fallen in love, telephone calls can be divided simply into two types: calls from "him" or "her" and every other call. You can make a further division. If the phone rings, it must be from "him" or "her." And if the phone doesn't ring for a long time, then people in love grow suspicious—it must be out of order. That's what love is.

    Love
    Means being captivated by the lyrics of the pop songs that flow from buses, from the street, from the radio. Especially sad songs. Sad songs create patterns of emotion in the hearts of those who are in love. People in love, consciously or unconsciously, long for parting, and very sad partings at that. That's why there are so many masterpieces among sad love songs. Pop songs allow lovers who long for parting but don't have the heart for it to have the experience vicariously. Pop songs may only be in fashion for a little while, but they don't disappear. They're a legacy handed down to those who've just fallen in love.

    Love
    Means being unable to walk by mirrors without studying your face. For the first time in my life I thought a lot about my face. I studied my eyes and my nose and my mouth without end. And I drew a conclusion. I thanked him for loving someone who looks like I do. He could have passed right by without loving me. I thanked him with all my heart for stopping, thinking this might be love. So love is a red light. When it's lit you have to stop. It warns of danger and promises safety. A red light. That's what love is.

11 A Fourth Memo about Love

*Nothing poisons love more than honesty.
If love lasts until the day we die,
We will live without showing our real
   self
To our beloved until the day we die.
Love makes us more beautiful and
   distorts us.
Love takes our impulse to lie to an
   extreme.*

F or several days after we came back, I clung to love. I knew this because I could not free myself from telephones, I was sensitive to pop songs, and I studied my face in the mirror for a long time.

Everything indicated love, a love that was a red light, warning of danger and promising safety. I was in love with Kim Jang-u.

But things weren't so simple. If I gave in a little to being illogical, I could see that my three memos about love also held good for my relationship with Yeong-gyu. And when I thought about this lack of logic, I realized it may just have been that all things needed was a little time. So I put as much time into investigating love with Na Yeong-gyu as I had put into confirming my love with Kim Jang-u.

First of all, there was no doubt that I felt no more freedom from the telephone in Yeong-gyu's case. Our relationship had continued to develop ever since that night when rain poured down onto the glass roof. The development was all in the direction of love and marriage, of course, and all of that was thanks to the services of the telephone.

To be honest, I'd consciously avoided meeting him since he proposed. I felt burdened by his demand to answer him as soon as possible. Every single time we met he'd ask me how I was coming along with my assignment.

"Can you answer me now? Come on, Jin-jin. Please. I'm ready to hear it."

But I was not ready. The big difference between the two of us is that I am slow at everything, and I had no choice but to keep on resorting to the same "Three Month Policy" I'd settled on to begin with.

"Please wait. I'm very slow. I need more time to think things over than you do." Since it wasn't an issue he could solve by making demands, he didn't press me further. Besides, Yeong-gyu is never pessimistic, and seemed to take it for granted that a woman needed three months on average to decide on a marriage proposal. I didn't want to drag it out any longer than that whether that was the average or not. At that point, I thought, everything would be clear—after all, a lot of things already seemed to be. Two months had passed and I was in the process of outlining my response.

Late at night, though, when we were talking on the phone, I'd suddenly be overcome by a suspicion that maybe I'd fallen in love with him as well. I felt much more at ease talking to him on the phone than meeting him in person. When I could talk to him without seeing his face, I was able to discuss all sorts of things openly. His voice, on the other side of the line, was warm and gentle. I could talk to him for hours about this and that as I sat at my desk, propping my chin up with my hand. At times like that, the thought that I could him marry him crossed my mind.

He would frequently call me late at night. I even took the phone into the bathroom with me out of fear that I might not hear it ring. Although I avoided his requests to meet, I would hold back from going out to the superette in front of our house after work just in case he called. Could this be love too?

That second memo about growing sensitive to pop songs applied in Yeong-gyu's case as well. Actually, that memo worked to his advantage. I would think about him when I listened to sad love songs. How would these songs make him feel if I break things off? They would turn into a sharp dagger and pierce his heart. I often imagined myself in his position and listened to sad love songs. Maybe this was love as well.

And if I really did a reckoning, the third memo about mirrors was much more remarkable where Yeong-gyu was concerned than with Jang-u. This was a truth I couldn't deny. As I said, I'm very ordinary, with nothing to boast about—the only thing I really have going for me is my age. I don't have the beauty that draws attention on the street, or a background that would make me a target to men. I'm not saying this because I feel embarrassed about it. It's just the truth.

So I felt very odd when Jang-u appeared first and began to open up his heart. Why was he doing this, I wondered? But gradually I began to think that such things could happen. In the sense that neither of us has anything to boast about, we are lovers who resemble each other as though we were drawn that way. Our love developed because he saw a version of himself in me and I saw myself in him.

It felt completely natural when Jang-u said he loved me, but when Yeong-gyu made his own confession, I felt uncomfortable, as if I were wearing clothes that didn't fit. At first I found it so odd that Yeong-gyu had stopped his tracks in front of me that occasionally I suspected an ulterior motive. He had integrity, a promising career, a wealthy family, and on top of it all, a bright, innocent smile. It seemed like a miracle that he'd laid his declaration of love at my feet.

So there really was nothing odd in my spending more time thinking about Na Yeong-gyu than Kim Jang-u when I studied myself in the mirror. I couldn't help but feel thankful that a man like him had made up his mind to love a woman as plain-looking as me. If gratitude like this is also love.

In spite of all the time I spent thinking it over, I couldn't find any definite hint that I loved Jang-u more than Yeong-gyu. I can say it easily now, but that thought caused me a lot of heartache. I was terrified that my pledge of last spring would come to nothing—my cry that I had to make every second of my life count, that life was not simply something to be accepted, but something to be lived in a spirit of adventure.

I wanted to fulfill the pledge of that day no matter what. If I didn't, I felt like I'd never be able to forgive myself for the pathetic life I'd led up to age twenty-five. Was my admirable resolve to hurl all my energy into the life that was given to me crumbling so quickly? As far as I was concerned, marriage was an important starting point to reach my goal. I'd chosen marriage among the many paths that were open to me at age twenty-five.

Please, do me a favor, and don't criticize me for making marriage my first choice. And don't try to use pretty words to convince me otherwise. Of course, I realize that women my age have other options and don't have to get married. Who doesn't?

But there are women who do choose marriage. Obviously there are others who study or throw themselves into their work or who scoff at marriage and travel around the world. It's not as though I'm the only one who hasn't examined the possibilities fully. I'm through with all this searching. Maybe my decision will be easier to understand if I say I made up my mind to seek the meaning of life in this particular way, because a life of deep reflection had grown awkward and that I'd wound up choosing a path that led to my hating myself.

I am who I am. We don't all have to live in the same way, but by the same token we don't need to kick and flail just to be different. I'd decided to stop being so harsh on myself. Instead of choosing a quiet, lonely path I'd take the road that many have gone before, because I believe that more of life's secrets lie buried beneath that universal road.

Still, my confusion about marriage and the complexities of love were making me suffer. That was a fact. But in the midst of all this I finally worked out an important clue about how to distinguish between the arrows I had drawn towards Yeong-gyu and Jang-u, and between love and what is simply like love.

Let me say first that the realization I had that let me work all this out may apply only to me. It could be different from my previous three memos on love that are universally true, but it was through this insight that I managed to sift out what was love.

Love starts with a desire to show a better self to our beloved and an effort to become "the way I want to be" rather than "the way I am." Nothing poisons love more than honesty. If love lasts until the day we die, we will live without showing our real self to our beloved until the day we die. Love makes us more beautiful and distorts us. Love takes our impulse to lie to an extreme.

I was honest with Yeong-gyu. The only thing I didn't tell him was that I was seeing another man. Other than that, I opened up to him about everything. He knew the reality of my situation, and I didn't find it especially painful to show all that to him.

But it was different with Jang-u. It may have simply been a little joke of fate that made me deceive him into thinking Auntie was Mom, but I found it painful to talk about my father, mother and brother to him. Reality always depressed him so I wanted to show him a more cheerful me, a more vivacious me, a more lovable me than actually existed. He was happy believing that my aunt was my mom—I couldn't confess to him now that she used to sell socks and now sold kimchi. I didn't want to say anything that might take away from his love for me. It wasn't at all because I feared his love would disappear when facts I'd kept hidden came to light. I know he's not like that.

But I couldn't hold back my desire to show a better me, even though it had nothing to do with preserving our love. That is love. I recognized it on our trip to the West Sea. My own worthlessness made me embarrassed before those scenes of nature, filled as they were with a sublime sorrow and a moving beauty. I didn't want to stride out to greet the love I'd waited for for so long wearing my shame like ragged clothing, especially not under the watchful blue eyes of the ocean.

We can show our worthlessness easily enough to those we're not in love with, but not in front of love itself. Love is proud.

That explained why I acted so differently in front of these two men. I was in love with Kim Jang-u. What I felt towards Na Yeong-gyu was merely a pseudo-love, some emotion that resembled love.

So the only thing left for me to do was to inform Yeong-gyu of all this. My three-month grace period was coming to an end. I still didn't know how I should tell him, what words I should use to console him. But, even now, as before, I remain grateful to him with all my heart for loving me.

矛盾

12 Unbearable, All Too Unbearable

*B*eing deprived of the chance
　To discover life's deepest secrets
Is a terrible thing
(If I may say so).
It is the misery of a patient on a
　special diet
Who has to eat the same thing,
Every day,
Day in, day out,
For his entire life.

One day in late November, when the weather forecast for the first snow of the year had proved wrong yet again, my aunt appeared out of the blue. The phone on my desk rang at 6:00 p.m. sharp, just as I was finishing work for the day. I picked it up hastily knowing who it would be.

"It's me, Auntie."

Not Jang-u. Taken by surprise, I was momentarily at a loss for words.

"You're about to get off work, right? Do you want to meet? I called because I thought it might be nice to eat together."

She sounded depressed. Although Jang-u might call, I couldn't turn her down. She'd called frequently to invite me over, but time had been flying by, and I'd simply forgotten about her for a while.

My aunt waited for me in a small park in front of our office. She was sitting on a cold cement bench with a wood pattern painted over it, and she was so lost in thought gazing at the cars passing on the busy street that she didn't notice me approach. It was the first time I'd ever seen her like that. I wondered if something had happened. Maybe it would be more precise to say that I wondered if something could happen to her.

"I really thought we'd have the first snow today. I came out in the morning to see it, but I've wasted my time again."

My aunt's dazed look vanished and she focused on me. As I saw her smile in her own particular way, I reconsidered. The worst problems Auntie faces are trifles like the weather forecast being wrong several days running about the year's first snow. One of the comforts in my life is knowing she's free from the pain of this shabby world.

"But it's still too early to give up, isn't it? There are still six hours to go before the day is over."

"Oh, Auntie. Is that all you wanted me for? You could have kept on the lookout for snow at home with Uncle. That would have been much more romantic. You called just because you wanted to wait for it with me?"

"Don't you like the idea? Did you already have other plans?"

I couldn't miss the shadow of disappointment that crossed her face. It was strange. That was how I always talked to her. It was just my way of saying that I was grateful to her for calling me. She had to realize that.

"Of course I don't like the idea. What's the point of seeing the first snow with your old aunt? A boyfriend, though, now that might be different."

I tested her again with our usual way of interacting.

"Really? Well, I guess there's no choice. I guess I'll have to look for some middle-aged romance of my own. I hope it snows today, if only so I can find a romance to keep forever."

My fears were groundless after all. I laughed with glee and she giggled. We clasped our arms together with confidence, like soldiers who had identified each other through a watchword.

"What shall we eat? What fits a day like today?"

We wandered around looking for something appropriate to have for dinner on a day when the year's first snow was wavering about whether or not to fall. We kept our arms tightly linked together, determined not to lose each other amidst the restless waves of people and the blazing neon signs that covered the street. The winter night was very pleasant as I walked with my aunt. There was a hint of perfume about her and her wool coat was soft and fluffy. Her body felt warm.

"It's nice."

"What is?"

"Walking with you in winter."

"I like it too."

"What?"

"Having a niece like An Jin-jin."

She looked at me and smiled sweetly. Her face was still beautiful, as was her smile. She held intact what my mother had lost long ago. When I was with Auntie, I couldn't help thinking about my mother. I didn't want to, but the associations were inevitable.

Mom finally opened her store, two months later than originally planned. At his final trial Jin-mo was sentenced to the term she'd been aiming for. It was the nicest present she'd received lately. The victim's affidavit, in which he repeatedly emphasized that the attack was not premeditated, played the decisive role. Of course, when I think about the money she invested to get that deposition, I have to agree that, as she put it, he bled us dry. Still, what else could she do? After all, to borrow her words again, "It's my flesh and blood that matters, not the money. I'm not worried about being able to earn a living anymore." Her life experience was a consolation to her, if you can call it that.

So it worked out that Jin-mo would be home by next winter at the latest. Mom finished reading her law books and went back to studying Japanese. Because of Jin-mo she never got to use that fall greeting she'd practiced so painstakingly. Instead she had to adopt "*Moo sorosoro huyu desu ne.*" So, winter is upon us . . .

Her store did less business than she had expected, because she'd been a step behind in opening up. According to her, between last summer and fall, several stores had already changed over to deal with the Japanese and they were taking the lion's share of the customers. To put it another way, she had to catch the last train because of Jin-mo. Nonetheless, it didn't bother her at all. It seemed to me that she'd become a woman of steel, a warrior in her dealings with the world. The first snow of the year held no interest for her. Life itself made so many desperate demands on her that she never had time to be bored.

Unexpectedly, Auntie made me swear an oath to her. "Never ever tell your mother that I called you to come out like this so we could see the first snow together."

She also seemed to be thinking of Mom.

"Think about Jin-mo for a second, having to spend the cold winter in prison. First snow . . . winter's on its way. Oh, I'm bad, I'm really a bad aunt. I shouldn't be doing this."

Her face burned with guilt. To my aunt emotion was reality. When she felt guilty, her face immediately turned red, and when she was sad, her eyes welled up with tears right away.

"It's okay, Auntie. Mom has done everything she could to make sure Jin-mo is comfortable. She's much better than I am at dealing with the world. I'm an idiot when it comes to that."

"Yes, you are a bit of a fool on that score. You take after me . . ."

She held my hand tightly in her coat pocket. Even though I wasn't her daughter, I did take after her a lot. Maybe if I were her daughter, I'd have grown up to be dull and rigid like Ju-ri. Being deprived of the chance to discover life's deepest secrets is a terrible thing, if I may say so. I realized that while watching Ju-ri. It is just like the misery of a patient on a special diet who has to eat the same thing, every day, day in, day out, for his entire life.

One of the managers at our company told me how he'd cried for three days when he was diagnosed with serious diabetes. I was taken aback at first by his confession because he had a huge frame and a fiery temperament. I didn't understand—he wasn't hopelessly ill. All he needed to do to keep leading a normal life was stick to the diet the hospital had arranged for him.

"You guys don't get it. I'm not allowed to eat until I'm full anymore, no matter how good the food is. That pleasure has been taken away from me. They warned me that if I eat more than a bowl of rice at a time I could die. And that's not the whole of it. They told me not to even bother coming to the hospital unless I quit smoking and drinking. I lived for that drink after work. My favorite foods are pickled seafood and vegetables, but they're an absolute no-no. And that's just the start. There are so many things I have to be careful about. The thought that all the pleasures in life had come to an end made me desperate. I guess I'll get used to it, but what am I going to do from now on? It would be easier to put up with if I never knew about all the great foods I'm missing out on in the first place . . ."

It was plausible enough that a change in diet could make this massive, middle-aged man cry for three days, so maybe Ju-ri would never have felt a sense of despair about what she's missing. Ju-ri grew up without ever knowing the possibility of other ways of life, without knowing of pickled seafood, so to speak. The world might have been able to firm her up, but the devoted protection of my aunt and uncle cut those opportunities off completely.

A monotonous life produces a monotonous happiness. The Ju-ri I met late last summer demonstrated this truth all too well. She taught me an important lesson. What makes us grow is not happiness, but the unhappiness we desperately try to avoid. It is always interesting to learn from observing other people. What offers more variations on a theme than human beings?

After a long debate about what food would suit the mood of the evening, my aunt suggested seafood spaghetti, and I agreed wholeheartedly. When you're wavering between choices, there's nothing as gratifying as another's insistence.

"Listen, I can't forget the taste of the spaghetti I had in Rome. It was slightly sweet, but also had a sour tang. I haven't been able to find anything like it in Seoul. I've even tried making it myself, but it always turns out wrong. How about if we try to challenge my memories of Rome again today?"

And so, I was able to tag along for a chic dinner and dream of a place I may never see.

"What was Uncle like in Rome? I know you must have acted like Audrey Hepburn."

"Uncle?" Her eyes went wide, as if questioning why I'd mention Uncle..

"Didn't you go together? When was that? You went on a trip to celebrate your twentieth anniversary, right?"

"Yes, right. Who else would take me to Rome? But I can't remember a thing about him being there. It's as though I went by myself. Is that strange of me?"

"I guess it would be the same for any couple that's been married twenty years."

I had no real idea what twenty years of marriage was all about, but I think I had a good sense what her trip to Europe with Uncle would have been like—Uncle, who defined success by how faithfully he carried out his obligations, and Auntie, who dreamed of the extraordinary. As I expected, she explained what he was like at the time with a sheepish smile.

"Oh, your uncle. He's finished wherever he goes, once he's taken three pictures—one of him, one of me, and one of the two of us together. Every night when we got back to the hotel he arranged his wallet according to how much he'd spent for the day and how much he thought he'd need for the next day and then fall asleep. He never even dreamed that I was pacing by the window all night, draining the liquor in the refrigerator bar."

My aunt was creasing her brow without realizing it. Maybe just like she did as she sat drinking whiskey at the window by herself? Or a sign that she resents her husband, boring now and boring then?

"Every night after we got back, he'd sit and arrange the photos we took in an album. My pictures, his pictures, the pictures of the two of us together. He put the three pictures with the same background on one page. Then, on the next page my picture, his picture, and the picture of the two of us together . . ."

She was still frowning. She kept talking as she wound and unwound the spaghetti on her fork.

"For a while after we got back he'd trot out the album every time we had guests over. 'This is the famous Spanish Plaza in Rome, this is the cathedral of Notre Dame in Paris, this is England—the Tower of London.' Even when the kids came home, the very first thing he did was drag out that album. 'This is the famous Spanish Plaza in Rome, this is the cathedral of Notre Dame . . .'"

As she spoke of a husband whose memories consisted only of photographs, she looked like a young girl who buys a storybook only to find it has a title but no text. It's empty. How strange.

"He doesn't even remember where I ate the spaghetti I liked so much, but as long as he has the photo album with the pictures side by side everything is fine with him."

She finally took her first bite from the spaghetti she'd been busily raveling and unraveling on her fork. I had already half finished. I waited for her opinion of its taste.

"Hmm. It's good. Similar. Probably because I'm eating with you. Everything tastes good when you're eating with someone you like."

I didn't ask who she'd been eating spaghetti with in the meantime. The probability of Uncle not being present was zero; I've never seen a husband who dotes on his wife more attentively. I hated to hear criticism of my uncle coming from Auntie's mouth.

I have to emphasize it again—Uncle might be boring, but he is not at all a bad person. Why criticize him just because he can't stand detours from the straight and narrow? Maybe the truth is I find it easier to snipe at my aunt's endless romanticism. It's much easier for me to scold her for that than to find fault with someone like Uncle. But then how can I account for my loving Auntie more than my own mother precisely because of that romantic streak? The endless contradictions of life—we wind up hating someone for exactly the same reason we took to loving them in the first place.

Actually, the spaghetti that my aunt had suggested for dinner and which I'd agreed to was very nearly a disaster. The seafood wasn't fresh and the tomato sauce was too sweet. I stopped eating after I had only about half of it. Auntie didn't even have that much. But she still maintained that the spaghetti we had was like what she ate in Rome.

"It was marvelous. I really like the décor in this restaurant. It's like the restaurant in Rome. The floors and the walls use the same light shade of wood."

I was glad that Auntie liked the place so much. Nevertheless, the world that greeted us after we finished dinner and coffee guaranteed more definite success. A flake or two of snow was falling, the year's first snow, just as my aunt's hunch had predicted.

"Look! What did I tell you? Today for sure!"

She couldn't hide her excitement. Judging from the way it was beginning to come down, it looked like it would be quite a substantial first snowfall.

"Great! I can feel happy now. I came to see the first snow and here it is in style. I'm going to treasure doing this with you, Jin-jin, until the day I die."

Still, I had a fleeting suspicion that that was just one of my aunt's slightly over the top expressions. Anything she liked became something she promised to treasure eternally. And the first snow was just the occasion to bring out her usual fussing. For a moment I glimpsed my mother's hyperbole in her, and I had the feeling that she was using it in the same way—gaining the strength to overcome life's miseries by magnifying them and kneeling in surrender to them. But I didn't have time to ponder all this, as Auntie said, "Let's walk, Let's just walk." She grabbed my hand with real urgency. "Quick. Let's hurry somewhere where there aren't too many people. It's no good here. The snow melts as soon as it lands. Come on!"

She seemed genuinely distressed to see the snow trampled underfoot. It was as though watching it disappear without a trace was the most painful thing she'd experienced in her whole life. I ran along the dark street clutching her warm hand as it grew damp. The snow began to fall more thickly above us.

It was a very strange night.

Even after I got home I couldn't shake the feeling that both the night and Auntie herself had been strange. I felt uneasy for a long time afterwards.

It wasn't a blizzard, but enough snow fell that night to satisfy everyone's expectations and allow them to enjoy the fresh whiteness that cloaked every roof until the next day. When my aunt caught a taxi to go home, though, there still wasn't any accumulation to speak of.

We couldn't find anyplace where snow covered the cold ground intact without footprints. We didn't realize it until we were out of breath and had to sit down to rest—or rather, that's when I convinced Auntie that we wouldn't find anyplace like that. I finally got the message through to her in spare moments as we dashed along that we were in the busiest area in Kangnam. The first snow meant that there would be even more footprints tonight, not fewer. Seoulites would be out in force, flocking to bars, restaurants and *noraebang*,[1] even on the back streets. My aunt, who had hardly been willing to believe me, stopped rushing a moment and looked straight at me.

"Okay, enough. Let's go home. I can just get a cab. I'm going to get going."

I couldn't believe it. She was thoroughly composed, as if everything we'd done up to that point had just been a joke. And, in fact, that's how her goodbye to me sounded as she got into the taxi.

"I had the most fun I've had in a long time. Thanks for coming out to goof around with your silly old aunt, Jin-jin. Bye!"

I felt ridiculous left standing there on the street amidst the falling snow. My aunt just wanted to come out and have fun; I felt like an idiot for getting myself caught up in all sorts of inferences and analyses. But something inside me insisted it wasn't all a joke.

There were three messages waiting for me at home, two from Jang-u and one from Yeong-gyu, but I didn't call either of them. It was too late to call Yeong-gyu and my thoughts were too complicated to call Jang-u. I thought that if I called him I wouldn't be able to keep myself from talking about Auntie. I'd have been perilously close to blurting out to him that I had been out running through the snowy streets with her and that I still felt strange, that she had bewitched me.

As far as Jang-u was concerned my mother was my aunt. I still hadn't broken the truth to him. When my mother came up in conversation, I was always careful not to destroy the image of Auntie as he'd seen her at the

---

1. The Korean equivalent of a karaoke bar.

French restaurant. I hated talking about Mom, but he enjoyed speaking about her a lot—or rather about Auntie, that is . . .

"Even though I just saw her once, I could draw her picture. Whenever I find myself wishing my mother were alive, it's always the image of your mom that comes to my mind. You look like her."

When he talks like that, how can I tell him after all this time that the woman he saw really wasn't my mother but my aunt? All I revealed to him—very cautiously—was that my mother had a twin sister. When he heard that, he became even happier.

"Wow! That's great. It must be like having two moms. Two stylish, loving mother figures? You're really lucky, An Jin-jin. The more I think about it, the more excited I get."

He was obviously speaking from the heart and wanted to know lots of things about my mother, as well as the father and brother whom I barely even mentioned. He expected me to talk about them—perfectly reasonably—just as he told me all about his only brother, but I still couldn't open up to him. But there will come a day when I can reveal everything to him—if we get married because we love each other, and if marriage then makes our love become as insipid as water.

My tale about my aunt and the first snowfall isn't finished yet, however. She wasn't one to leave an episode in which she had appeared hanging with so many loose threads. She needed to put the finishing touches on it. My puzzled headshaking, my thoughts that it had been a strange night, proved that I didn't understand my aunt well.

"Have you eaten yet, Jin-jin?"

I'd just returned to my desk from lunch break when Auntie's resonant voice greeted me on the phone. If she'd put off calling me just one more minute, I'd have dialed her number myself. My co-workers and I had been talking about the snow at lunch, and I made up my mind to call her as soon as I got back to the office.

"I was just about to call you . . ."

"Did you make it home okay? Come on, ask me too, 'Did you get home all right last night?' "

I had a vivid picture of her smiling and felt relieved that obviously nothing had happened to her.

"You didn't just go straight home last night, did you?"

As soon as I asked, my aunt launched into a report of what she'd done after we parted, as though she'd been waiting. Her voice was bright and sunny.

"With the snowflakes coming thicker and collecting in people's hair and turning it white? How could I just go home? I got off on the way."

She told me how she walked for ages when she got out of the taxi. It was late at night and there were few people around to leave footprints, so she was able to enjoy the crunch, crunch, crunch of fresh snow beneath her feet all she wanted. She had a hot cup of coffee, sitting at the window of a cafe that spilled soft yellowish light out onto the street. Then she went into a record store and purchased a CD, and finally she bought seventeen sweet potatoes from a young street vendor who was roasting them.

"Seventeen?"

"Yes. Seventeen. I bought them all up. He said his girlfriend was waiting for him. They had a pact about the first snowfall. They were going to rendezvous at a special place that only the two of them knew about. He was positive she was waiting for him, so I told him to go hurry and meet her."

I laughed loudly. What a brilliant assault on my aunt's romantic streak. Fantastic. She obviously had been tricked, but I told her she'd done well. It was like the tired story old countryfolk might use, how they came to Seoul looking for their son, but couldn't find him and now had to sell the honey they'd brought as a gift. Evidently these lines had been updated by a new generation.

"This was the first time in my life I've seen a first snow as beautiful as this and it'll probably be the last. It was really great."

Finally she brought last night's encounter to a conclusion. I suddenly pictured my aunt's living room, too big for her to sit alone in. Was she looking out at the traces of snow in the yard? She said she bought a CD last night—I wondered what song it was that she liked these days. I perked up my ears. Sure enough, there was music in the background.

"Are you listening to the CD you bought last night?"

"Uh huh. I've been playing it over and over again all morning—it's great. I bet it's all I'll be listening to for a while now."

The song she adored so much even after listening to it again and again was called "The Day after We Parted." It was especially its title that she loved—it sent a chill up her spine. It was time to hang up, and I made a casual joke as a way of saying goodbye.

"So who was it you parted with, Auntie? If you're having an affair, I don't even want to know. I wouldn't be able to deal with it."

"Jin-jin, I'm really curious. What would it feel like the day after parting? How would time pass for me? Would it be so hard to bear I'd feel like dying? I'm really curious, really, really curious."

"Auntie, my gosh, the day after you part with who? What kind of man are you talking about?"

"What kind of man? You want to know what kind of man? Your uncle, of course."

"What? Auntie, you can't . . ."

"It's a joke, silly. A joke. Okay, I'm hanging up now. Bye."

She really is too much. I chuckled to myself for a long time after our conversation was over. My darling, mischievous aunt . . .

My fondness for Auntie made me decide to let myself be infected by her fever, so after getting off work, I found a record store and bought a CD with Yi Hyeon-u singing "The Day after We Parted." I also bought her a new album containing Jo Yong-pil's "Song of the Wind." It was the sort of song she'd like. Maybe she even already knew it, but it didn't matter. Someday after a big snowfall, I'll visit her, my head sprinkled with white. She'll probably be surprised and say, "Jin-jin, I'm going to treasure this gift forever and forever, until the day I die. That's a promise . . ."

13 The Day After We Parted

*Yesterday morning was not like this.
Everything was fine.
This morning when I opened my eyes
Everything had changed.*

December arrived.
A winter rain replaced the snow and made the streets wet and dismal for a few days. When night fell the potholes would freeze over, only to melt again during the day. A thin layer of ice is even more slippery than a real sheet of it. Every morning I walked to work with my eyes fixed on the ground so I wouldn't lose my footing.

"Turn off the boiler. I'm burning up."

What Mom found hardest to put up with since the start of winter was the sound of the boiler. I humored her by keeping the thermostat set as low as possible. It was inevitable I'd feel sorry for Jin-mo, stuck in prison over the winter. Thoughts of him would come to me abruptly—when I waited at the bus stop, stamping my frozen feet, or when I would turn up my collar to ward off the stinging cold settling into the back of my neck. Jin-mo was always uppermost in my mind whenever I was somewhere cold, rough, irritating.

And one day something happened I'd never once imagined—the dove, Jin-mo's dove, flew into our house. I had no interest in Jin-mo's women and had never given her much thought. You might think I resented her just a little bit since it was because of her that Jin-mo went to prison, but that wasn't the case at all. Even if there had been no dove, Jin-mo would have followed his own path. Everything on his path had already been planned. The dove was just a stepping stone for him on his way to the dark authority, the boss's dignity that several prison terms would confer. And a stepping stone, just like the name implies, could be substituted for by another at any time.

But here she was, a discarded stepping stone. I couldn't help being astonished. It was Sunday morning, and Mom had already gone to the market. The chime of the doorbell was thin and hesitant. I opened the door to find a girl with a small, childlike face standing there.

"Are you . . . An Jin-mo's sister?"

Tears began welling in her eyes with that question. A single word from me, and they would have tumbled in colossal drops.

"I'm . . . Yun-hui. Because of me, Jin-mo . . ."

The tears began making their way down her pale cheeks.

"I came to beg for forgiveness. . . Please forgive me."

I was speechless. Jin-mo had compared her not just to a dove, but to a dove shivering in a cold rain. A single glance told me this was obviously who he meant. I took a step back and silently signaled her to come in.

I led her to my room, not because I intended to be so warm and welcoming, but because we couldn't talk in the vestibule, which was as cold as if it were outside. Even afterwards Yun-hui the Dove did nothing but cry silently. I found it bizarre that she could cry so much without a peep. Like a tap that has been set to a trickle, water flowed out without affecting the muscles of her face at all.

"Please stop crying. What's the use?" As she was my younger brother's girl, I spoke to her in a mixture of polite and plain styles.[1]

"I was wrong. Please forgive me. Jin-mo said he can't. I went to see him several times, but . . . it was no use. . . Please help me. How can I change his mind? . . . Please help."

I had nothing to say. This was the first time in the course of Jin-mo's love life that a woman had betrayed him and then come back begging to be forgiven. Is this what girls his age are like these days? Is it even possible for a girl these days to be like this?

"You saw Jin-mo?"

"I went lots of times . . . but he doesn't say anything. He just said to go back and that he wished me the best. . . He said he doesn't love me anymore. . . What should I do? I still love him. I was wrong. I did get interested in someone else, but it was just for a really, really short time. I'll never do anything like that again . . ."

"Do what Jin-mo says."

As soon I said that, she shrieked and grabbed my knees.

"No! Please help me!"

She's, what, twenty years old? She acted like a little kid. I could tell immediately that she'd been able to get whatever she wanted throughout her young life by crying. She had an appealing fragility about her, and she knew it. Man, it would be hard to stay cool in front of a girl like her, I thought. I also thought how elated Jin-mo would be if I went to see him soon and passed on

---

1. Korean verbal endings indicate the relative social status of the speakers and can easily convey respect, formality and distance or their opposites. Because of the situation, Jin-jin uses a mixture of styles to address Yun-hui.

the news about her. As I looked at her, the image of the *chaebol* family roster kept scrolling before my eyes.

"Yeah, I figured as much."

Jin-mo wasn't at all surprised when I told him what had happened. He acted as though he'd been expecting it. He looked different somehow, but his health didn't seem to have suffered. Actually, his complexion looked even better than when he was at home—proof of how well Mom had been topping up the food he got in prison. The beard he'd grown made it hard for me to read the thoughtless expression hidden beneath it.

"All that because of her, and she's already yesterday's news?"

"Yun-hui has to go her own way. That's better than screwing up her life clinging to a guy like me. I pray that she'll be happy. From the bottom of my heart."

I didn't buy a word of it. He might be able to use his voice to create a gloomy atmosphere, but he can't fool me. I could tell immediately that the dove hasn't finished her role. Jin-mo hadn't cast her aside completely. Sure enough, the *chaebol* family register was exerting its power.

"Do you sound so forlorn when you talk to her too?"

"Yeah. I say to her that if you truly love someone you have to set them free. And I told her to give up this kind of life and to keep studying, like her parents want. 'I won't see you again,' I said, 'but you're the only one I'll ever think about.' I promised to protect her even in her dreams."

If you keep repeating a lie often enough, eventually you can't even tell what's real anymore. That's what had happened to Jin-mo. He'd been taken in by his own words, and now he was becoming choked up.

"So you're going with melodrama this time."

"Huh? Melodrama?"

"Yeah, just like in those old tearjerkers. I can tell you're trying to keep her hooked, but be careful. She seems to be into this school of acting. And she can be quite the refined little lady, just like you say. Well, good for her, but I feel sorry for my younger brother. You look a little pathetic, trying to act like Mr. Cool."

"Don't worry. I know how to deal with girls like her better than you do. When I made up my mind to thrash the guy who took Yun-hui to within an inch of his life, I counted on a day like this. I got a little scared at first because I thought he really had bought it. Why the hell did those idiots of mine go so far overboard? But everything is going okay now, just the way I want it. Be nice to Yun-hui if she goes to see you again, because I really might marry her. I'll have a hard time finding a better girl."

Jin-mo was confident. His tone might have been on the point of changing once, but throughout, his voice dripped with a beautifully tragic melancholy. The heavy atmosphere he created almost overwhelmed his surroundings. It's what gave me the feeling there was something different about him as soon as I saw him. I gave up. Even as he was confessing to shameful secrets, he used a feigned tone rather than a natural one, unaware of the difference. When it became impossible to tell the two apart, what was the point of even trying? Now he had no other way of living left.

But I wasn't completely honest with Jin-mo either.

Go ahead and say I have no conscience, but I still hadn't been able to tell Yeong-gyu that I loved someone else. I admit it.

And you can call me shameless, but I had yet to give him the slightest inkling that the wedding might come to naught. That was the situation when his company sent him off to Japan on the second of the month for a two-week training course.

I was waiting for D-day now, as it were. The polite thing would've been to tell him if I didn't want to force him to do extensive remodeling on his grand life plan. He left for Japan in a state of anticipation.

"You're going to have a terrific gift for me when I get back, won't you?"

Yeong-gyu didn't realize that bitter gifts existed as well. In a sense it would have been much easier to say goodbye to someone like Jang-u, who was prepared to accept pain, than to Yeong-gyu. But it was Yeong-gyu I intended to say goodbye to.

"Maybe I should wait a few more days and have your answer as a Christmas present. That's a good idea. We can spend an unforgettable Christmas Eve together. It'll be great."

I was going to have to say goodbye to a man who called all the way from Japan to plan a splendid exchange of gifts.

Yeong-gyu had been waiting long enough. He had respected my wishes, but only as far as he could without it interfering with his life plan, and that made me feel less guilty. I knew that he loved his plan more than he loved me. Nothing in his life, no matter how important, could be allowed to deviate from it. Love was no exception. Everything was fine for him if he could love someone within the plan's limits. Why try to find someone outside them?

While Yeong-gyu was in Japan, Jang-u moved back to his brother's apartment. Well, strictly speaking, his brother's family moved in with him— Jang-u took the money from the deposit for his work space, together with his savings and an advance on the royalties from his publishing company, and rented an apartment just big enough for all of them. According to Jang-u, now that his brother had a place to live, he was thinking of setting up as a small-time trader doing business with China.

"He'll do well. Not just with China, but anywhere. He's been an expert on China ever since he started his travel agency."

Jang-u kept reassuring me that his brother would succeed, as though he felt guilty about having emptied his purse for their apartment together. Jang-u was thinking about his marriage funds. So was I. But I'd have done the same thing if I'd been in his shoes, and I wished that I was rich so that the man I loved wouldn't feel so guilty. I became even more close-mouthed about my family's poverty. I had no choice. I couldn't tell him what was really going on, how my mother didn't have any regular customers because she'd jumped on the bandwagon too late, how sick she was of her ever-increasing stock and fussy Japanese customers. If you spill your guts about everything, love becomes dirty. Love does not want honesty.

"But I'm happy these days, An Jin-jin. Every night I get to wash Jang-ho's smelly socks without my sister-in-law knowing . . ."

And so we postponed our wedding plans indefinitely until we could get together enough money for a room for the two of us—not that we said so explicitly, but we'd come to a tacit agreement about it. It's how people live who don't have concrete plans like Na Yeong-gyu. Going about life this way has its conveniences—you can revise things on the spot. If it doesn't work out, change. And if that doesn't work out, change again. And if that doesn't work out . . .

And while I was still trying to figure out what to do if things didn't work out, Yeong-gyu returned. He called me as soon as he arrived at the airport, and suggested we get together, even if just for a minute. That day we were having an end-of-the-year office party that I couldn't get out of, and he had no time the following day.

"Okay, let's just meet on Christmas Eve the way we originally planned. I can wait. How about you? Let's see, I'm going to have to hurry up and make reservations if we want to do something really special. It'll be tough if I don't."

Yeong-gyu set the date and hung up. I remained clutching the phone for a long time, unable to set it down. I felt strange, as though I was doing something wrong, a suspicion that this was not what I wanted. My doubts stayed with me even after I put the receiver back.

His words stayed with me. It'd be tough to do something really special without reservations. Was there some important truth about life that I was missing?

I didn't fall asleep until very late. I listened again and again to the song my aunt had recommended—or rather, the song that had captured her, "The Day after We Parted." I must have listened to it dozens of times. In the end I was able to sing along with it without having seen the lyric sheet.

> How was your day today? Were you okay?
> Any regrets? Getting ready for your next date?
> Not everyone can be in love, I guess.
> Today has been so, so long, now that you've left me.
> Yesterday morning was not like this. Everything was fine.
> This morning when I opened my eyes, everything had changed.
> Can't you take my heart that loves you away with you?
> Today has been so, so long, now that you've left me.
> Can't you come back like nothing has happened?
> Did you love me?
> Please just tell me you did.
> Are you leaving me?
> I can't do anything.

What will I feel like the day after Na Yeong-gyu and I part? How will he feel the day after we part?

I lay on the floor with my chin propped up in my hands, thinking hard as I listened to that sad song over and over again. This isn't my song. I can't say for sure, but maybe this would be Yeong-gyu's song in the near future.

And I had another thought. Pop songs are right about love, if about nothing else. They might not convey any truths about life, but they convey truth about love. So this song is not mine . . .

矛盾

14 Christmas Present

Life is short.
But all its hardships
Make it long.

P eople don't put much thought into the way they talk about the unexpected. "I knew it was coming. I had a premonition about it . . ."

But real happenings are always sudden. Even when people know something can actually occur, they don't believe it'll happen that day or the next. There is no today or tomorrow in premonitions, only "some day." But every day is a today or a tomorrow.

My father came back.

I knew he would, but I never believed it'd be today or tomorrow. And I certainly didn't expect he'd return on Christmas Eve, as if he'd promised me that's what he'd do.

"It's me. Can you come home now if you don't have anything important?"

A few minutes after lunch a call came from my mother. I could sense she was trying to calm herself down. And just as I was thinking how strange it was for her to ask me to come home now, all of a sudden my father's face popped clearly into my head. Dad?

"Your father has come home. Please come as fast as you can."

Yes, Dad. He had come back.

Leaving work early was easy enough. The period around New Year's was our company's down time; for about ten days before and after Christmas importers can't do a thing. My heart pounded as I straightened my desk. Dad's return wasn't completely unexpected, but it had happened in an unexpected way.

It had been five years since I'd last seen him. He came as if he were a house guest, stayed for a few days and left as he had come, a house guest. I didn't see him go. When I went out in the morning, my father was lying there alone, staring at the wall. When I came home late at night after my part-time job, my mother was lying there alone, staring at the wall. My father had handed the warm spot, the best spot on the floor for lying and staring at the wall, over to her and left. Not a word about whether he'd come back a year later, or perhaps in two.

What would be as futile as asking my father when we'd see him again? He could return—or not return—at any moment. Such things didn't concern him. At some point back then, the matter stopped concerning us as well, the family that was left behind. Guest are guests in the truest sense only if they arrive unexpectedly.

But were we really so indifferent? I found it hard to shake off the unusual tone in Mom's voice. She wasn't one to call and ask me to come home early. I'd have been able to see my father in the evening. The unspoken agreement he had with us was that if he came home he stayed at least two nights. It was as though he needed that much time to release his pent-up paternal affections.

The front gate was open, and Mom was sitting on the edge of the vestibule. She still hadn't taken off the heavy winter coat that she wore to the market. As soon as I walked through the gate, she led me quickly back out to the alley. But before she ushered me off, my gaze landed on my father's shoes, stowed neatly beneath the wooden floor. They had been worn far too long—nothing of their original shape remained. The toes curved stiffly toward the sky, and the heels had fallen to pieces. My father's shoes.

Ah, nothing captures how Dad looks as clearly as those shoes do. Those cast-off shoes summed him up neatly. The reality of his return finally sunk in, but I could feel in my bones that he'd be leaving again. If not, he wouldn't be my dad.

"Something's wrong with your father."

Mom certainly wouldn't have said that if he'd simply arrived suddenly as before, an unexpected guest, who planned to stay a few days and then go. She ignored my questioning look and just stood, arms folded, staring at our neighbor's wall for a long time. Her silence was an omen of some new disaster. Finally she delivered the news, like a judge pronouncing a heavy sentence.

"He must've had a stroke at some point."

I couldn't say a word. I was too busy trying to wrap my head around the idea that he was old enough to have had a stroke.

"Plus his mind is all over the place. I think he's got Alzheimer's on top of it."

Again, I found myself speechless. A stroke and Alzheimer's at his age . . . he may have been a wanderer who had escaped from the inevitable ways people live, but he couldn't escape the inevitable diseases of old age.

"It's heartbreaking to look at him. You wouldn't even think he's human. When he came into my shop, at first I thought I'd seen a ghost. Everybody in the market came out to gawk at him—that tells you all you need to know."

Mom's hyperbole was slowly kicking into gear. I was relieved. That meant a solution was also in the offing. I knew her well.

"Things are going to be a mess today and tomorrow because of Christmas, but I'd better take him to the hospital right after. His condition is going to do nothing but eat money, but what other choice is there? He's the father of my kids and I can't just chase him away."

As expected, Mom was already preparing a conclusion. I went into the house first. It was quiet inside. The old shoes below the veranda were the only sign that my father had come home.

"He had a few shots of *soju* and now he's sleeping like a log."

Mom's voice, cracking, followed me as I opened the door. It was dark inside the room; soon it would grow dark outside as well. My father was lying on the warm spot on the floor, just as he had five years ago on the day he left for the last time. It was as though those five years had never taken place.

But when I saw his face from close up, my sense of familiarity was obliterated. The way he looked made it seem that time had carved out a river of not five, but a full fifty years between us. His cheekbones protruded through his haggard skin, and dark age spots were spread among his drooping wrinkles. His greying hair was as tangled as a pad of steel wool.

He slept like a corpse, his breathing the only sign of life. Mom was right. This old man who had collapsed here so tragically was not my father.

This was not how the father of mine who returned home every few months or years used to look. His lonely homecomings during melancholy sunsets had a charm that can't be put into words. He would come in with darkness at his back, the evening wind tousling his black hair. His dark pupils would glimmer from within his deep-set eyes, and at every movement the faint scent of far-off places wafted from within the wrinkled folds of his trousers . . .

A foul smell permeated the room. I slipped out. Mom was already wrapping herself up in her scarf to go back out to the market.

"I . . ."

I was on the point of telling her that I had to meet someone that night, but I just closed my mouth. Mom had put on such warm, bulky clothing she looked like she'd been rolled into a snowman. With a troubled expression on her face, she headed out to do battle once more. Best if I said nothing.

"Stay here and keep a close eye on him. Watch the stove too—I'm boiling down some soup stock. I was in such a state that I left the shop wide open. Today of all days, too, when there are so many customers! . . ."

She didn't seem as energetic as when she had Jin-mo's troubles to contend with. She grumbled continuously and appeared distracted. Her lips were agape, not clamped shut like they should have been.

"What a disaster. Why can't he just go off somewhere and die quietly? How much more of my juice is he going to sap? People in that condition don't just croak!"

People in that condition don't just croak! Her exclamation was as determined as if she were memorizing an incantation that would give her strength and left. As her cry echoed in my head, the phone rang. I hurried over to it, afraid it might wake my father.

"Hi, An Jin-jin. It's me."

As soon as I heard Jang-u's voice, the desperation I'd kept bottled up inside came welling to the surface.

"I tried to call you at work, but they said something had come up at home."

How much had I told him about my father at that point? I hadn't revealed every last detail, but I hadn't lied. I must have told him about what my father had been like until I turned five or six, how he quit his job and then had had a hand in various small businesses, running an auto repair shop for a few months and a tiny printing house for another few, how he always just started a business, but was too afraid to throw himself fully into it, no matter what. That's the extent of what Jang-u knew about my father.

"My father is very ill."

I massaged my chest, trying to settle myself down, and told him very briefly what had happened.

"I see... That's too bad... I'm sorry..."

Jang-u was not good at offering words of comfort. Unsure what to say, he asked if it was all right to come and visit my father.

"There's really no need. But cancel our visit to your brother's tomorrow. It's going to be difficult."

"Okay. Don't worry about it... That's fine."

My plan had been to spend Christmas Eve with Yeong-gyu, turn his marriage proposal down gently, and then go to Jang-u's brother's house on Christmas Day and meet his family formally. At last I'd thought I could predict the course of my life, but now another postponement?...

I had to call Yeong-gyu. He'd already informed me yesterday about every last detail of what we'd be doing today.

"I've got two presents for you, but don't get me wrong. A single word is the only gift I need from you, so don't get worked up about buying anything. If you come with a pretty smile on your face, that'll be plenty. Okay?"

Yeong-gyu, who had no idea what I was thinking (well, to be more precise, who had not even once tried to guess what I was thinking), was as jolly and cheerful as ever.

Chapter 14 Christmas Present

After his call yesterday I thought of that famous story, "The Gift of the Magi." A husband sells his watch to buy a comb so his beloved wife can make her beautiful hair even more shiny and beautiful. His wife, though, cuts off her golden tresses and sells them to buy a fashionable chain to go with the watch her beloved husband cherishes so much. The presents this poor couple prepared by selling what they treasured most became useless. As I thought about these touching Christmas gifts, I felt tremendously guilty about Yeong-gyu. That presents in this world could be so moving but go at cross-purposes . . .

Yeong-gyu sounded obviously upset with me for breaking our date. It was the first time that had happened, and his anger made it hard for me to continue. He'd been just on the point of going out to our meeting place, and demanded an explanation as to what on earth had come up. I had a clear image in my mind of his round face becoming square.

It was odd, but the way he was acting suddenly put me at ease, and that sense of comfort let the grief I'd been burying emerge. Setting my mind at rest, I had a good cry. I sobbed, feeling relaxed before him. I'd been strong in front of Jang-u, who didn't know how to console me, and I'd wanted to remain strong. It was really odd.

"Jin-jin, what's wrong? Tell me. Don't just cry. Tell me what's the matter."

He was perturbed, but I felt his reaction was anxiety that something serious had come up with the woman named An Jin-jin that might spoil his Christmas preparations. He wasn't worried about me, so much as having the date he'd prepared for so carefully be cancelled. I cried harder, not deliberately, but to expel the wail that was caught in my throat. To be honest, deep down I was waiting for his anxiety to turn into irritation. It would only be real life when that happened, I thought.

"Okay, we'll meet next time. Please call me."

Once Yeong-gyu learned that my father had come back seriously ill and transformed almost beyond recognition, he chose his words very carefully. He knew that my father stayed away from home for long periods. Finally he had to admit to himself that his return meant there was no way around canceling our date.

All the research and analysis, the reservations and reconfirmation that had gone into planning today's chic event had fallen to pieces.

"I'm sorry."

"Well, there's nothing that can be done about it. Really, there's no end to the problems at your house. And I went to a lot of trouble for those reservations . . ."

At last Yeong-gyu gave a hint of annoyance. The remark included a jibe at what had happened to Jin-mo as well. It was a perfectly natural thing to say. He was just being himself. I couldn't go on forever begging Yeong-gyu's tolerance about a family in which exceptions were more common than rules.

But it really was okay with me, because I believed I didn't love him and I wasn't going to marry him.

As I went off to the kitchen to check on the soup that was boiling down for my father, I stopped in my tracks. Was it all really okay? I didn't love Yeong-gyu, but he said he loved me. I again firmed up my resolve to turn down his proposal, but he'd already made it clear long before that he wanted to marry me. I felt okay, but it wasn't okay for him.

How can I explain it? I couldn't sit still now that I'd been captured by the idea that I was okay, but that Yeong-gyu absolutely could not be. I couldn't respect myself at all. I had to tell him the truth quickly. I rushed to my room and dialed his number, giving no thought to the idea that I might be spoiling his Christmas.

"Ah, Jin-jin. I just cancelled the reservations . . ." He sounded delighted to hear from me, as if he'd been expecting me to call.

"You did the right thing. I have something to tell you. Are you busy?"

"It's okay—the office is completely empty. I'm the only one left." His tone told me he'd gotten his hopes up only to have them dashed again.

"My dad's condition means I'm not going to have time to meet you for a while. You know I'm the only one to take care of him. And there's Jin-mo's situation too."

I made a point of reminding him about Jin-mo, but not out of anger. As long as I didn't have to see his face, I could say anything to him. "I wouldn't be sorry about making you wait for a long time if I had a nice present for you, but I can't make you wait if I have to pass on bad news."

I could sense obvious traces of his tension in his silence and went on. "I would've been able to tell you easily today, because it's not just something I've been thinking about for a day or two. But then this came up. Maybe it's better this way. I was really worried about having to say all this in person."

"What do you mean? You can't be saying . . ."

"Yes, I have a bad present. I've thought a lot . . ."

"Jin-jin, hold on a second!" He cut me off quickly. "Are you saying these things because I got annoyed just now? I'm sorry. But you shouldn't speak so harshly. Now I can see that you've got a mean streak. How about we meet and talk about things when your father is better? Don't get caught up in the emotions of the moment, okay? Let's just stop here."

And then he really hung up. I found a fast busy signal mocking me, as my mouth was still open, about to continue with my next words. An absurd thought came to me—well, that's sure one way to avoid bad news. The strategy had never occurred to me before.

The complications of my life overwhelmed me, but my father didn't stir for a long time as he unloaded the exhaustion of his own life in slumber. Outside all was busy, but on Christmas Eve our house was plunged into deep quiet. A silent, almost holy night.

What better day to return home after wandering the world as a missing person? I know people say that life is short, but all its hardships make it long. My father had truly lived a long life. The question was, had it really been the life he had wanted?

I sat at his bedside without turning on the light. I wanted to be there when he opened his eyes. I wanted to be the first thing he saw when he woke.

Inside the room a scarlet glow lamp reflected off the floor and cast a dim light over everything. My father would be able to recognize me easily. Over twenty years ago he'd given me the name Jin-jin, using the character for "truth" written twice. But he'd also bequeathed to me the fateful family name "An," which denied it. How much time did I occupy of all the many hours of his wanderings? Had thoughts of me at a melancholy setting of the sun ever moved him to tears?

The cover of darkness tends to make people sentimental. As I sat beside him, the idea came to me to take his outstretched arm and finally measure my hand against his. We will recognize each other only when our hands matched exactly, he'd said. If they don't match, we'll be doomed to live sadly without knowing that we're father and daughter. Keep your half of the secret well until then.

But somehow, I couldn't bring myself to actually do it. Several times in my head I went over grasping his wrist and stroking his palm, but before I could finish my mental rehearsals, my father suddenly jerked awake back from sleep to the world of reality. I immediately saw the changes my mother had spoken of.

"Wh-who are you?"

His first words were a frightened question about my very identity. Who am I? Who is An Jin-jin? Instead of answering, I turned on the light. Both my face and my father's aging, withered visage revealed themselves clearly. But he still didn't recognize me.

"Wh-who are you, miss? I must have done something wrong again. . . Oh, please forgive me, if I did."

He hastily rose from the bedding and stood, bent at the waist, trying to guess what I might be thinking. Legs trembling, he flapped his gaunt wrists about, unsure where to let them rest. His lips curled upward on the right side, and he watched me with a craven look in his eyes.

I cried. I'd reached a peak of love for the father I remembered, but the man who had actually arrived made a cruel mockery of my memories. I had waited so long. This was unfair. I left the room, wiping away my tears with the back of my hand. He hurried out to the porch after me.

"Where am I? How did I get here? Are you the owner of the house, miss? Could I . . . could I get just a spoonful of rice?"

Not sensing any particular hostility from me, my father's instinctive response changed. He moved from fear to shamelessness in an instant, beaming as he asked for a bit of rice. My tears continued to fall as he exposed his yellowed teeth in the sweetest smile he could muster.

矛盾

15 Bittersweet

Even too much love
Is worse
Than not enough.

I had no choice.

I couldn't leave Dad alone for even a moment so I got permission to take leave without pay for the slow month of January. It was an everyday event for him to limp away from the house in nothing but his underwear. When I peeped into his room because it was too quiet, I might find him taking a match to some toilet paper and trying to light a fire.

At the hospital they just shook their heads as well. The palsy that had stricken his right side had already set in firmly, and his senility would only grow worse each day. I met a woman there who was helping to look after a patient in her family. She emphasized again and again how her own mother had lived for ten years in such a state. I couldn't tell whether to take her words as sympathy or a warning.

When my father was admitted to the hospital at the end of last year, I was told that Auntie and Uncle had visited him, even though I didn't see them. My father. Sick, miserable, helpless, with darting eyes and no sense of shame. It pained me horribly to think that this was the figure he presented to my aunt and uncle after so many years.

There was no more snow after that first heavy fall, so I hadn't met with Auntie since then. I intended to run over to her house the next time it snowed to give her the CD as a present, but I just locked it away in a drawer.

"Your aunt is looking really skinny. She says she keeps getting sick." As Mom passed on the news, she added, "She's a crybaby. With all her good luck you'd think she'd act differently."

The flesh of the winter watermelon that Auntie bought for us was red and sweet. My mother dug in with more gusto than my father did, but she didn't forget to season the fruit with bitter remarks.

We ushered in the new year at our house by putting a fist-sized lock on our front gate. It was a depressing way to start the year. Sometimes my father became lucid, but I never saw him that way. It only happened when he was alone together with my mother.

"Early in the morning I had a strange feeling and opened my eyes. There was your father, staring down at me while I was sleeping. I was startled out of my wits. But he's completely with it then. He even makes perfect sense when he talks . . ."

Mom didn't tell me what he said to her when he was in his right mind, though. I didn't pry, despite my curiosity. In any case, I could tell from the way she was acting that she'd already forgiven him when he came back, even if she didn't come out and say so. Yes, she shouted at him and made him tremble when he did something ridiculous. And no, she hadn't forgotten her hyperbole and still used choice vocabulary when she talked to me about him. But she was also slowly gathering her strength, as she did with Jin-mo.

The proof lay in her reading. She had gone from *The Understanding and Treatment of Schizophrenia* to Japanese conversation books and then made a sudden turn to stiff law texts. Now she had returned to medical books with titles like *How to Treat Palsy* and *Alzheimer's, The Disease That Destroys the Family*. Not only had she forgiven my father, she refused to abandon him.

Maybe I hadn't given up on Dad either. I'd insisted on taking a month's leave even before my mother suggested it. And I was the one who suggested we tell Jin-mo only about his palsy, and not the dementia that was making him go downhill so quickly. I thought that, like me, Jin-mo would be able to accept that Dad was half-paralysed, but that he'd find his senility much harder to take.

But the person whose details needed to be kept hidden was not my father, but Jin-mo. When I went in Mom's place to visit him and tell him as calmly as I could that Dad had returned, his face turned bright red. My father had witnessed Jin-mo just barely complete a checkered school career, drifting from one high school to another as a delinquent, and then he went his own way for the last time.

"Did you tell Dad I'm here?"

Jin-mo put the question to me carefully and tried to read my expression. His beard had grown in nicely since I'd last seen him. Now anyone would recognize him as a high-ranking gang member.

"Did he ask about me? Look for me? Just say I got a job down in the provinces. I'll tell him the rest. There's a lot I want to say to him."

A lot to say? Jin-mo's longing for Dad seemed greater than his anger towards him. His words were fraught with meaning. Had Dad also shared with Jin-mo the secrets of life that only he knew? Probably, because I'm sure he loved his son just as he loved me.

One day in January, when the market was closed and Mom was able to stay home to take care of Dad, I kept the promise to meet Jang-u that I'd been postponing. I bought a bouquet of red roses and a cake and went to his apartment. There he was with his brother, sister-in-law, two nephews and a small puppy. The space was too cramped for a large family to live in together with Jang-u, but everyone looked so happy that it put me in a good mood for the first time in ages.

No one there, puppy included, had the slightest doubt that I'd also become a family member in the not too distant future. I could tell at a glance that his brother was a good person, and his sister-in-law was gentle and generous. They both began calling me Sister then and there, as though I was already part of the family.

The wedding plans that Jang-u had never mentioned to me were clear enough in his brother's words. Apparently, we were getting married in the spring, and during our honeymoon days we'd be living in a small apartment nearby. Traces of austerity all over their home made it obvious just how carefully they were saving to get together the key money for our apartment. I was touched. Likewise, even though I was visiting for the first time, we made do with barbequed pork. Jang-u's sister-in-law said, "What's the point of eating beef now? Better to have it later once you and Jang-u get married."

The scene was picture perfect—brothers who loved each other more than their own lives. Jang-u turned to look at me every time his brother said something, as if asking me to feel as much affection for his brother as for himself, and to forgive him if his love for his brother was deeper than his love for me.

But suddenly I could see my own father's face in Jang-u. Overwhelming love can be dangerous—my father was unable to handle his and fled for good. Perhaps fate was preparing a life for Jang-u that he could not imagine. Who knows? Even if one were to know, there'd be nothing that could be done about it. Even too much love is worse than not enough.

My sweet An Jin-jin. My sweet, sweet An Jin-jin . . .

That day as we were returning from his brother's, somewhere in the dim alley near my house, he planted kisses on my forehead, my nose and my lips, repeating those words as if reciting an incantation. Bittersweet kisses.

矛盾

16 A Letter

*By the time you read this letter,
I will probably be gone.
Please come to me,
Come and take care of me . . .*

D on't come too soon or too late.
If I look ugly in the end, please fix me up.

So ended the letter I received from my aunt. It was a dreary February day, with brooding grey skies. The mercury had been dropping steadily, as if determined to freeze the world.
I don't know how I can talk about what happened. It's hard for me, no matter how I steel myself. My hands shake, and tears blur my vision.

Exactly ten days after I returned to work from my month's leave of absence, a small package appeared on my desk at three in the afternoon when I got back from the president's office.
"Miss An, express package for you," someone said.
I was indifferent up to that point, without the slightest sense of foreboding. Three o'clock in the afternoon, an hour when disaster was not even a blip on my radar screen. And then a bolt from the blue. A letter that flew in and cut through that languid hour. How could this happen?
Auntie.
Two syllables. That was the entire return address. I still suspected nothing. It was the first time she'd ever mailed me a letter or package, but I should have realized that wouldn't be how she'd fill in the return address. She would've perfumed her words—"Auntie, who misses you" or "Your beloved aunt." I'd received presents and cards signed like that from her before.
An Jin-jin.
If I'd looked closely, I'd have realized at once that every stroke of the lettering in my name was too stiff. The ink was applied in layers and showed clearly that she'd addressed the package to me slowly. An. Jin. Jin.

Two keys and an envelope with a letter tumbled out. Keys in a package? Auntie must be playing some sort of practical joke. I snorted a small laugh.

I ripped open the envelope, eager to see what delicious conspiracy she was cooking up this time. My rough movements tore the white stationery inside. I never could have dreamed that blood flowed within.

My aunt's letter, the first and last she ever wrote me, began affectionately. "Jin-jin."

Jin-jin.

I've spent so much time over the last several days thinking and thinking about writing you a letter. But now that I am writing it, I'm so exhausted I don't have the strength to remember everything I wanted to say.

It was easy to decide to send this letter to you. I feel very sorry about that, but no matter how hard I tried I could not think of anyone else. You will be able to come up with the excuses about my life that I cannot. I felt that I would not be embarrassed, if it were you . . .

I

Am going to end it now. It has just been too difficult.

I really have no answer if you ask what has been so difficult. That seems to be my tragedy. I've found it all too difficult, but I have no words to offer about my difficult life. My life was smooth when I was a child, and as I grew up. When I met a man and got married, it became even smoother. A tedious life that blocked me completely from experiencing any sort of need.

So I'd like to end it.

I've always been bored. Your mother's life has been busy. She had to earn money all day long, fight with a scoundrel of a husband, and hunt after children who ran away and then give them a sound thrashing. Her life had to be so hectic that the wind always whistled around her. I envied her so much. I wanted to live a real life too, not one that was as quiet as a tomb.

I often imagined springing up from this tomb and leading a real life. But it was not easy. I was locked within a fortress. If I tore down the fortress walls, many people would have been hurt. I can't stand the thought of so many people being hurt just because of me, but I also can't stand the thought of living quietly like other people. No way.

Jin-jin, I can't cope with either option.

I've decided to end things now.

I realize all too keenly that living takes more courage than dying. But I have no courage and I'm a fool. I know that if I were in some major accident in which several people were injured, I would not wind up on the list of survivors. So let's just consider my death an accident.

Jin-jin.

Chapter 16 A Letter

Please forgive me for leaving you to deal with the aftermath of all of this. By the time you read this letter, I will probably be gone. Please come to me, come and take care of me... Uncle won't be back from his business trip until later. I doubt I'll be wrong. I'm not good with numbers, but I worked out the timing very carefully. I even asked at the post office. Believe me, I don't want to make any mistakes in this last act.

I hope you will make excuses for me to Ju-ri and Ju-hyeok. They told me that they have decided to live over there when they graduate rather than coming back. If I'm gone, they will be able to forget this land more easily. I don't resent them. I resent myself for not being able to live like them...

Jin-jin.

Don't come too soon or too late.

If I look ugly in the end, please fix me up.

How could I have even begun to imagine I'd ever receive a letter like this, that Auntie would send me such a letter?

As I ran to my aunt's, I kept praying to myself over and over, please, please, God, let this just be a joke. Please, I beg you, make this letter a joke!

I flew off to her house without contacting anyone. I believed—no, I wanted to believe—that it was a joke. I was afraid that if I made a fuss or told anyone that it would all come true. I was so determined to make sure it didn't come true that I had no room to think of anything else.

And yet, it was not a joke. I opened the gate with one of the keys and the porch door with the other. The eerie silence that greeted me made me realize at once that it was no joke. In the dim living room the curtains dangled peacefully, as in a painting. They shut out the rest of the world. My aunt lay motionless beneath them, stretched out on her back.

I don't remember how I acted after I found my aunt lying there dead. I do remember horror overwhelming me for a moment when I realized I was too late, but then I thought about the letter. I remembered I had a task to take care of before I did anything else.

If I look ugly in the end, please fix me up.

There was nothing to fix up, nor was there any trace of agony. After she'd straightened everything, she had come to the window to look out over the outer world and take her last breaths and then she flew off forever to a faraway place. Something to fix? Only one thing. Her death.

Next I called my mother. No sooner had she answered than she disappeared with a single shriek. I could tell she'd fainted from the sounds of commotion at the market coming over the receiver she had dropped. But I couldn't run to her. I had to watch over my sad aunt lying under the window.

Before darkness enveloped the world, my uncle arrived, ahead of my mother. Everything was proceeding precisely according to my aunt's calculations. He ran to her, pushing me away as I cried, my whole body trembling.

"Why? Why? Darling, how could you do this?"

All through the funeral ceremony and after the burial, he remained racked by a sense of betrayal. It was as though he knew no other words to say.

My mother arrived next. I'd never seen her so pale. She rested her head on her sister's chest and cried in weak, gasping sobs. She fainted several times, and this time there was nothing exaggerated about what she did. I realized that my mother and my aunt shared one body, although this was not clear because they'd become so different. Two people with one body and different lives. I understood my mother's sorrow as the pain of having one half of her own body fall apart.

Ju-ri and Ju-hyeok barely made it back in time. They arrived just as the funeral procession was on the point of leaving, and did not even get to see their mother in her final state. Ju-ri grabbed hold of the coffin as it was being loaded into the hearse and wailed, shaking.

"Mom, forgive me, please forgive me . . . There was no other way. Please understand, even in death—"

As we were in the car on the way back from the burial, Ju-hyeok told me that Ju-ri had fallen madly in love with a young professor. "He's American, of course. It must have been a real shock to Mom. She hoped we'd come back, but we had our own lives to lead. I refuse to believe that's why she decided to kill herself. She wasn't that foolish."

I acknowledged that as well—she was not foolish. Except for choosing death over life, the Auntie that I knew was truly a wonderful woman. And I can even understand that. This world is too shallow for someone like her to take root in it and thrive.

Thus my aunt departed. For three days, the sky was gloomy and the late winter wind was extremely harsh. My head felt dry and grainy, filled with sand. I was in a daze and phrases from her letter kept running through some corner of my mind.

Jin-jin, I'm going to end it now . . . It has just been too difficult . . . I wanted to live a real life too . . . not one that was as quiet as a tomb.

On the day everything was over and I left my aunt's, I found a few CD's scattered on top of the stereo. I looked through them one by one, the songs that touched her heart. Among them was "The Day after We Parted."

矛
盾

17 Contradictions

*O*nce upon a time lived a smithy,
A seller of spears and shields.
Boasted he to the people,
"This spear smites all shields."
Again said he,
"This shield parries all spears."
Immediately pried the people,
"And if spear and shield should collide?"
The smithy simply fell silent.

Even after Auntie died, time flowed on.
The winter that stole her away came to an end. Spring ripened, the scent of flowers everywhere. If there is winter, there can be spring.
I went on living in accordance with the passage of time as well. You can die only if you live. I still can't understand such contradictions, but I can accept them. Life and death conspire with each other. We shouldn't be deceived.

The trivial stories of the living continue.
Until death, nobody can put an end to life's insignificant episodes. We go ever forward, hanging the hours that have passed in various picture frames, large and small.
My uncle is doing well. The enormity of Auntie's immense betrayal wounded him, but it couldn't stop his train in its struggle to arrive and depart on time.
Ju-ri celebrated her wedding with a blue-eyed, brown-haired man in the United States. She sent some wedding photos to Mom. In them she smiled brightly, fully the bride. When I looked closely, though, I could see that she had a smile on her lips, but no joy in her eyes. Her mother's death must have been both the greatest and the only pain she's experienced. Through her death, Auntie has prevented her children's lives from becoming completely tedious. Ju-ri and Ju-hyeok will reflect upon it for the rest of their days.
Jin-mo is still confined within both a prison cell and the world of idols he's constructed so solidly during the brief course of his life.
One of life's trivial incidents happened to Jin-mo even while he was in prison. The dove finally departed. Taking Jin-mo at his word in his declaration of an unselfish love, she flew off with tears in her eyes to study in Australia, where one of her sisters had already settled. Jin-mo was heartbroken—he hadn't suspected that his dove would fly so far away so soon. Grief made him

so haggard and worn that Mom was worried sick. If the dove had stayed in Seoul or gone to Busan, he'd have been able to send out his minions to take charge of the situation, but Sydney was too far. Jin-mo understood that if he couldn't control her, she'd take up roost in a new nest immediately. He also knew that the dove he'd captured and lost belonged to an expensive breed the likes of which he'd never see again.

Nonetheless, his dream of becoming a stylish gang boss has not disappeared. He hasn't given up the belief that if he keeps up his efforts, he'll win himself a worthy moll. And so, Jin-mo remains imprisoned, still speaking in low tones like Choe Min-su and giving icy looks à la Marlon Brando.

Jin-mo may never escape from his world, where fantasy and reality coexist in equal measure. Who knows? Maybe after a lot of time has passed, reality and fantasy will be reversed. Utterly and completely.

Mom has stayed as happy as ever. My father, now bedridden, has to be wiped clean of his excrement and babbles constantly, but he keeps her from becoming bored. Her son, who shows no sign of having developed any sense when she visits, likewise helped her life from lapsing into tedium. I became noticeably silent and would shut myself up alone. My depression also made my mother happy.

Mom hired a helper for her shop because she needed to take care of Dad. But having to pay out the helper's salary with little revenue also has filled her daily existence with tension. She has become busier and more energetic with each passing day. Ah, Mom's life, happy and unhappy . . .

My father freed himself from the constraints of his own life long ago. Now he's living on borrowed time. He enjoyed his real life on his own and has come back at last to share what he's received as a bonus. He's now the epitome of simple innocence. All the conflict and suffering experienced by someone who has seen the other side of life became nothing when squeezed into a single quality—all that remains is an enormous appetite.

The only thing my father's brain waves react to with any liveliness is food. Several times a day he carries on about dying of hunger.

"I'm starving. Oh, I'm starving to death. Look! My belly is stuck flat to my backbone!"

My father, who used to speak to me of melancholy sunsets and share beautiful secrets, has vanished. I confirmed this by bringing his hand together against mine. They didn't fit—his hand had been shrunk by age and disease. I eagerly spread open his gaunt, bony fingers and put my palm against his. My fingers were a half-inch longer, even leaving aside how much thicker and fuller they were. And so, even now he still doesn't recognize me.

Maybe we'll part for good without ever having recognized each other, and without me ever getting to ask why he stayed away from his beloved family and wandered. Perhaps that was the important secret of life that he wanted to pass on to me.

>Once upon a time lived a smithy,
>A seller of spears and shields.
>Boasted he to the people,
>"This spear smites all shields."
>Again said he,
>"This shield parries all spears."
>Immediately pried the people,
>"And if spear and shield should collide?"
>The smithy simply fell silent.[1]

Now it's my turn.

I'm getting married soon. Like my mother and my aunt, I'll become an April bride, although not, of course, on April Fool's Day. One morning about a year ago I woke up suddenly and cried out, "I've got to make every second of my life count. That's exactly what I have to do!" I've finally reached the stage of putting that pledge into practice through marriage.

For a year I devoted myself to my pledge. I examined and thought through things as much as I could. I've made a decision. Yeong-gyu is going to grasp my hand in that April wedding ceremony, and so the song "The Day after We Parted" will belong to Jang-u and me. I'm different from my aunt, though. She thought the day after parting meant only death. I endured it well; I have no way of knowing how Jang-u felt.

People need unhappiness as much as happiness. My aunt's death taught me that you can really live only when you always, if possible, have equal measures of both. Given what I learned, it would've been right for me to grasp Jang-u's hand.

But her death made me let go of his hand. Her life looked blessed to everyone, but she was miserable. Likewise, my mother looks miserable to everyone, but she was blessed in my aunt's eyes. All that remained for me was deciding what kind of happiness and unhappiness to choose.

I chose what I don't have. I decided to seek from Na Yeong-gyu what I clearly lacked before and what I would have continued to lack with Kim Jang-u.

Even if I wind up in the tomblike peace that my aunt found unbearable, I can't avoid it. You can never fully heed any of life's lessons until you have

---

1. Readers should note that the word "contradiction" in Korean (*mosun*) derives from Chinese, and the characters of this compound mean literally spear and shield and suggest their clash with one another.

experienced them viscerally. Even though we know that fire burns, we still draw closer. A contradiction, but one that will make me grow. I believe that. There's a saying that preaching to the deaf is like "reading the classics into the ears of cattle." Everyone has cattle ears.

One last thing.
I want to revise what I said a year ago.
Life is not something to live as we investigate it—life is something to investigate as we live it. Mistakes repeat themselves. That's life . . .

矛盾

Afterword
Contradictions–Seeking Life's Secrets

1

After I completed the final revisions of the manuscript and sent it off to the publisher, I got around to straightening up the mess on my desk. As I was doing so, I suddenly came upon my notebook—the notebook I always keep on my right throughout the many hours of the writing process, the notebook that acts as a receptacle for my excess flow of words.

Sometimes as I'm busily typing away, continuing on with the story, sentences come to me suddenly. They go strutting around in my head. They have nothing to do with what my fingers are tapping out at the moment, but they very much deserve to find their way into what I will write or what I should have written. They are not sentences I as author have created and are absolutely not to be missed. Someone—not me—is beaming out words that have been set aside precisely for this work. That's what I believe.

And so, the handwriting in my notebook is extremely hard to decipher. I can't take the time to put finishing touches on these phrases if I want to record them before they are lost. If they do slip away, I simply can't continue to work until they have been recovered. Once I wound up in tears because I couldn't recapture them, despite all my efforts.

I have a slightly embarrassing confession to make. After I finish my tooth-and-nail struggle with my novel, I sit and flip through my notebooks, feeling a vague emptiness in my heart. And all the hours that have passed seem like a dream. So much so that I can finally put an end to my constant self-reproaches for not living like a real human being and forgive myself a little. This is the only time when some leniency is allowed. Occasionally I even act as my own advocate: you have no choice but to live this way. Don't be so hard on yourself.

2

A look through my notes reveals that *Contradictions* differs slightly from my other novels. My previous notebooks are simply full of memos pertaining to the movement of the narrative. That is, they contain words that came to me just before the novel was written, words that only needed to be entered into their appropriate place within the story. As I muse over them this time, however, I find items that look out beyond the story, thoughts in my own voice, divested of the clothing of fiction, words from the author that are properly uttered outside the confines of the novel. For this reason they were unable to find their way naturally into the novel and remain scribbled notes, like lost orphans.

I decided to find a proper home for these words. I revised my intention to keep my afterword brief in spite of myself; instead, I've decided to be briefer with the authorial remarks expected of me elsewhere, in interviews and the like.

As always, I feel awkward about these authorial "pronouncements" that I'm supposed to make with a serious expression on my face. I don't know how other writers feel about discussing their creations elsewhere, rather than just letting their creations speak for themselves, but for me it is not merely difficult, it's embarrassing. As far as I'm concerned, "truth" is like a hot soup that needs to cool down a bit before one can eat it. And that means that in writing, truth goes with constant revision.

3

The first memo unrelated to the storyline that I came upon in the notebook was an incomplete sentence: "Hoping people read slowly, very slowly . . ."

I jotted that phrase down when I'd written half the novel. Only rarely do I find myself thinking about future readers, let alone muttering orders to them while in the throes of writing. I'd always felt that no matter how readers understood a novel, their various interpretations broadened the dimensions of the text.

Contradictions differs in several respects from my other works. To begin with, this was the first time I started to write a novel without serializing it. Up until now, the most direct spur to my writing has been a deadline, together with a specified story proposal. Without the two, my repeated polishing and revision might have kept many of my pieces from completion.

Even though the absence of a deadline meant I could throw away what I'd written or procrastinate at will, I kept my promises to myself faithfully, or nearly so. While I was writing *Contradictions*, I accepted no further manuscript proposals. It was the first novel I wrote with the sense of abundance that comes from complete devotion to a project. I neither had to produce an installment on a monthly basis, nor did I try to write other pieces at odd moments in the midst of it all.

Absolute devotion had previously only been possible for me with short stories. Novels take several times as many hours to craft, and I found it extremely difficult to keep up a consistent sense of tension from beginning to end in working on them. Moreover, as a genre, the novel requires a great deal of description in order to set up a structure for the narrative. In parts you have to speed up or slow down the story to create a proper flow or insure that its various parts are well integrated.

Nevertheless, I decided to give up the small benefits that go with writing a novel this time. I made an effort to tackle *Contradictions*, insofar as possible, with the spirit of utter concentration that goes with short stories instead. And so, I did not receive that little bonus of being able to add a single extraneous page to the work. Superfluous bits are apt to slip in to a lengthy manuscript whether you want them or not, but that didn't happen with *Contradictions*. I paid a high price in writing it.

Human nature makes us less attached to what we receive for free. We appreciate items in direct proportion to their cost. I was contemplating how one could read a book so as to treat it with real value, and thus I could not help jotting down, "I hope people read this novel slowly, very slowly."

4

Happiness and unhappiness, life and death, body and soul, wealth and poverty. Such pairs of antonyms crop up frequently in my notes for *Contradictions*. If you want to point to the mental patterns that underpin the novel, you will find them in these scrawled words.

For quite a while now I have been unable to simply pass over pairs of words that run counter to each other. There must be a reason, I thought, why a concept is inevitably bound with its opposite. I threw out a question to myself: don't writers have the task of expressing this reason in universal terms?

Contradictions was an answer to this question, and thus it was only natural for the story to feature twin sisters. I couldn't pursue two opposing lives by positing a single person with only one life to live. I thought identical twins the most appropriate device to show the traces of one life that is two, of two lives that are one. As I was roughly halfway through the novel, however, I had an important insight: we are all of us, every single human being, identical twins. Our appearances and personalities may differ, but given a single inversion, I can be you and you can be me.

It may seem abrupt to stress this point, but we all live our lives to the extent that we have interpreted them. And to expand our interpretative possibilities, we should not content ourselves with the dictionary definition of a term. We should look up its antonym as well. Happiness lies opposite unhappiness, and vice-versa. If you poke around behind wealth, you will encounter poverty; behind poverty lies hidden the wealth we were unable to discover. The antonym that supplements a dictionary entry is no different from a twin sibling.

5

Let me get a bit more serious at this point. I can't avoid it. The remainder of the jottings in my notebook that did not pertain directly to the story were queries for myself, random thoughts all pointing toward a single question: what is a writer?

A writer is likely to encounter that question frequently. During my twenty-year career, I've been asked it countless times as well. And during the course of those twenty years, my answer has changed countless times, although I would not say the change has involved transformation on my part. Let me take that back. It has been a transformation. My answer necessarily relies on how I've lived as an author and how I've written. "What is a writer?" The question demands an answer that takes into account a writer's entire life.

What, then, is a writer? The answer I'd probably give you at this point is that writers are those who devote their lives to creating a new reality within a novel, a new reality that transcends the given limits of human life.

I have always firmly believed that fiction, by virtue of being made up, is the art form that allows us to reflect upon and contemplate the one life we have. I've never departed from this basic principle either when I read other authors or when I am writing myself. Therefore "narrative" and "emotive force" have been my central concerns in fiction.

To put it another way, I, as a writer, have clung to "narrative" and "emotive force" as principal subjects. The world an author dreams of is one in which narrative transcends life's limits and the sensations created by a new reality can be shared. Unfortunately, accomplishing the two simultaneously is not easy; therein lies the writer's agony.

And so, I'm not only indifferent toward, but skeptical of, all discussions of fiction that ignore "narrative" and "emotive force." Likewise, I don't think

I trust theories that champion only "narrative" *or* a form of "emotive force" based on analysis. Such theories hold no place for the author. Theories of the novel that take into account neither author nor authorial spirit nullify at once the birth of the genre of the novel.

These days I find myself thinking again about how the writer's spirit can strip away the rags of daily life and help assuage a sense of loss.

6

A novel is not completed once it has been written and the book has been bound. If it is not read, and no moments of active interchange between readers and text occur, it remains unfinished. The one thing an author desires during the writing process is these moments of active interchange, for only then is the novel completed. Propped up by that one desire, writers thrust away the world's temptations, compose themselves and create fiction.

When expert readers' impressions of a work get into circulation, they foster biases, regardless of whether the impressions are friendly and sincere or harsh and violent. These biases can all too easily become enemies that snatch away an author's desire, a reader's sensation, and the work's own opportunity for completion.

While writing *Contradictions*, I dreamed that every member of the novel's audience would be a "first reader." I wanted to encounter the pure impressions of a first reader, unsullied by other impressions about the work that were circulating.

7

I hesitated a great deal over what to call the novel. I thought an abstraction like *Contradictions* rather heavy for the title of a work that treats the most concrete realities.

I soon changed my mind, however. If we look into our lives, we find that everything is a mass of contradictions. Theoretical truth and the truths that exist inside our thoughts don't always point in the same direction. *Contradictions* is a statement about life and about human beings who run smack into a wall of contradictions no matter what path they choose. The world is made up of contradictions. When we come closer to understanding them, we come a little closer to understanding the essence of life. No title, then, could be more concrete.

8

These days, when the world has changed so abruptly and when people are anxious and bewildered, what can a work of fiction give us?

I wanted to offer a word of comfort to those who are losing courage and have taken a tumble. That is the real reason I wrote *Contradictions*.

Summer 1998
Yang Gui-ja

CORNELL EAST ASIA SERIES

4 Fredrick Teiwes, *Provincial Leadership in China: The Cultural Revolution and Its Aftermath*
8 Cornelius C. Kubler, *Vocabulary and Notes to Ba Jin's Jia: An Aid for Reading the Novel*
16 Monica Bethe & Karen Brazell, *Nō as Performance: An Analysis of the Kuse Scene of Yamamba*
17 Royall Tyler, tr., *Pining Wind: A Cycle of Nō Plays*
18 Royall Tyler, tr., *Granny Mountains: A Second Cycle of Nō Plays*
23 Knight Biggerstaff, *Nanking Letters, 1949*
28 Diane E. Perushek, ed., *The Griffis Collection of Japanese Books: An Annotated Bibliography*
37 J. Victor Koschmann, Ōiwa Keibō & Yamashita Shinji, eds., *International Perspectives on Yanagita Kunio and Japanese Folklore Studies*
38 James O'Brien, tr., *Murō Saisei: Three Works*
40 Kubo Sakae, *Land of Volcanic Ash: A Play in Two Parts*, revised edition, tr. David G. Goodman
44 Susan Orpett Long, *Family Change and the Life Course in Japan*
48 Helen Craig McCullough, *Bungo Manual: Selected Reference Materials for Students of Classical Japanese*
49 Susan Blakeley Klein, *Ankoku Butō: The Premodern and Postmodern Influences on the Dance of Utter Darkness*
50 Karen Brazell, ed., *Twelve Plays of the Noh and Kyōgen Theaters*
51 David G. Goodman, ed., *Five Plays by Kishida Kunio*
52 Shirō Hara, *Ode to Stone*, tr. James Morita
53 Peter J. Katzenstein & Yutaka Tsujinaka, *Defending the Japanese State: Structures, Norms and the Political Responses to Terrorism and Violent Social Protest in the 1970s and 1980s*
54 Su Xiaokang & Wang Luxiang, *Deathsong of the River: A Reader's Guide to the Chinese TV Series Heshang*, trs. Richard Bodman & Pin P. Wan
55 Jingyuan Zhang, *Psychoanalysis in China: Literary Transformations, 1919-1949*
56 Jane Kate Leonard & John R. Watt, eds., *To Achieve Security and Wealth: The Qing Imperial State and the Economy, 1644-1911*
57 Andrew F. Jones, *Like a Knife: Ideology and Genre in Contemporary Chinese Popular Music*
58 Peter J. Katzenstein & Nobuo Okawara, *Japan's National Security: Structures, Norms and Policy Responses in a Changing World*
59 Carsten Holz, *The Role of Central Banking in China's Economic Reforms*
60 Chifumi Shimazaki, *Warrior Ghost Plays from the Japanese Noh Theater: Parallel Translations with Running Commentary*

61 Emily Groszos Ooms, *Women and Millenarian Protest in Meiji Japan: Deguchi Nao and Ōmotokyō*

62 Carolyn Anne Morley, *Transformation, Miracles, and Mischief: The Mountain Priest Plays of Kōygen*

63 David R. McCann & Hyunjae Yee Sallee, tr., *Selected Poems of Kim Namjo*, afterword by Kim Yunsik

64 Hua Qingzhao, *From Yalta to Panmunjom: Truman's Diplomacy and the Four Powers, 1945-1953*

65 Margaret Benton Fukasawa, *Kitahara Hakushū: His Life and Poetry*

66 Kam Louie, ed., *Strange Tales from Strange Lands: Stories by Zheng Wanlong*, with introduction

67 Wang Wen-hsing, *Backed Against the Sea*, tr. Edward Gunn

68 Brother Anthony of Taizé & Young-Moo Kim, trs., *The Sound of My Waves: Selected Poems by Ko Un*

69 Brian Myers, *Han Sŏrya and North Korean Literature: The Failure of Socialist Realism in the DPRK*

70 Thomas P. Lyons & Victor Nee, eds., *The Economic Transformation of South China: Reform and Development in the Post-Mao Era*

71 David G. Goodman, tr., *After Apocalypse: Four Japanese Plays of Hiroshima and Nagasaki*, with introduction

72 Thomas P. Lyons, *Poverty and Growth in a South China County: Anxi, Fujian, 1949-1992*

74 Martyn Atkins, *Informal Empire in Crisis: British Diplomacy and the Chinese Customs Succession, 1927-1929*

76 Chifumi Shimazaki, *Restless Spirits from Japanese Noh Plays of the Fourth Group: Parallel Translations with Running Commentary*

77 Brother Anthony of Taizé & Young-Moo Kim, trs., *Back to Heaven: Selected Poems of Ch'ŏn Sang Pyŏng*

78 Kevin O'Rourke, tr., *Singing Like a Cricket, Hooting Like an Owl: Selected Poems by Yi Kyu-bo*

79 Irit Averbuch, *The Gods Come Dancing: A Study of the Japanese Ritual Dance of Yamabushi Kagura*

80 Mark Peterson, *Korean Adoption and Inheritance: Case Studies in the Creation of a Classic Confucian Society*

81 Yenna Wu, tr., *The Lioness Roars: Shrew Stories from Late Imperial China*

82 Thomas Lyons, *The Economic Geography of Fujian: A Sourcebook*, Vol. 1

83 Pak Wan-so, *The Naked Tree*, tr. Yu Young-nan

84 C.T. Hsia, *The Classic Chinese Novel: A Critical Introduction*

85 Cho Chong-Rae, *Playing With Fire*, tr. Chun Kyung-Ja

86 Hayashi Fumiko, *I Saw a Pale Horse and Selections from Diary of a Vagabond*, tr. Janice Brown

87 Motoori Norinaga, *Kojiki-den, Book 1*, tr. Ann Wehmeyer

88 Chang Soo Ko tr., *Sending the Ship Out to the Stars: Poems of Park Je-chun*

89 Thomas Lyons, *The Economic Geography of Fujian: A Sourcebook*, Vol. 2

90 Brother Anthony of Taizé, tr., Midang: *Early Lyrics of So Chong-Ju*
92 Janice Matsumura, *More Than a Momentary Nightmare: The Yokohama Incident and Wartime Japan*
93 Kim Jong-Gil tr., *The Snow Falling on Chagall's Village: Selected Poems of Kim Ch'un-Su*
94 Wolhee Choe & Peter Fusco, trs., *Day-Shine: Poetry by Hyon-jong Chong*
95 Chifumi Shimazaki, *Troubled Souls from Japanese Noh Plays of the Fourth Group*
96 Hagiwara Sakutarō, *Principles of Poetry (Shi no Genri)*, tr. Chester Wang
97 Mae J. Smethurst, *Dramatic Representations of Filial Piety: Five Noh in Translation*
98 Ross King, ed., *Description and Explanation in Korean Linguistics*
99 William Wilson, *Hōgen Monogatari: Tale of the Disorder in Hōgen*
100 Yasushi Yamanouchi, J. Victor Koschmann and Ryūichi Narita, eds., *Total War and 'Modernization'*
101 Yi Ch'ŏng-jun, *The Prophet and Other Stories*, tr. Julie Pickering
102 S.A. Thornton, *Charisma and Community Formation in Medieval Japan: The Case of the Yugyō-ha (1300-1700)*
103 Sherman Cochran, ed., *Inventing Nanjing Road: Commercial Culture in Shanghai, 1900-1945*
104 Harold M. Tanner, *Strike Hard! Anti-Crime Campaigns and Chinese Criminal Justice, 1979-1985*
105 Brother Anthony of Taizé & Young-Moo Kim, trs., *Farmers' Dance: Poems by Shin Kyŏng-nim*
106 Susan Orpett Long, ed., *Lives in Motion: Composing Circles of Self and Community in Japan*
107 Peter J. Katzenstein, Natasha Hamilton-Hart, Kozo Kato, & Ming Yue, *Asian Regionalism*
108 Kenneth Alan Grossberg, *Japan's Renaissance: The Politics of the Muromachi Bakufu*
109 John W. Hall & Toyoda Takeshi, eds., *Japan in the Muromachi Age*
110 Kim Su-Young, Shin Kyong-Nim, Lee Si-Young; *Variations: Three Korean Poets;* trs. Brother Anthony of Taizé & Young-Moo Kim
111 Samuel Leiter, *Frozen Moments: Writings on* Kabuki, *1966-2001*
112 Pilwun Shih Wang & Sarah Wang, *Early One Spring: A Learning Guide to Accompany the Film Video* February
113 Thomas Conlan, *In Little Need of Divine Intervention: Scrolls of the Mongol Invasions of Japan*
114 Jane Kate Leonard & Robert Antony, eds., *Dragons, Tigers, and Dogs: Qing Crisis Management and the Boundaries of State Power in Late Imperial China*
115 Shu-ning Sciban & Fred Edwards, eds., *Dragonflies: Fiction by Chinese Women in the Twentieth Century*
116 David G. Goodman, ed., *The Return of the Gods: Japanese Drama and Culture in the 1960s*

117 Yang Hi Choe-Wall, *Vision of a Phoenix: The Poems of Hŏ Nansŏrhŏn*
118 Mae J. Smethurst and Christina Laffin, eds., *The Noh Ominameshi: A Flower Viewed from Many Directions*
119 Joseph A. Murphy, *Metaphorical Circuit: Negotiations Between Literature and Science in Twentieth-Century Japan*
120 Richard F. Calichman, *Takeuchi Yoshimi: Displacing the West*
121 *Visions for the Masses: Chinese Shadow Plays from Shaanxi and Shanxi*, by Fan Pen Li Chen
122 S. Yumiko Hulvey, *Sacred Rites in Moonlight: Ben no Naishi Nikki*
123 Tetsuo Najita and J. Victor Koschmann, *Conflict in Modern Japanese History: The Neglected Tradition*
124 Naoki Sakai, Brett de Bary, & Iyotani Toshio, eds., *Deconstructing Nationality*
125 Judith N. Rabinovitch and Timothy R. Bradstock, *Dance of the Butterflies: An Anthology of Nara and Heian* Kanshi
126 Yang Gui-ja, *Contradictions*, trs. Stephen Epstein and Kim Mi-Young

Order online: www.einaudi.cornell.edu/eastasia/CEASbooks, or contact Cornell East Asia Series Distribution Center, 95 Brown Road, Box 1004, Ithaca, NY 14850, USA; toll-free: 1-877-865-2432, fax 607-255-7534, ceas@cornell.edu